The Case of the
Six Bullets

The Case of the
Six Bullets

R. M. LAURENSON

COACHWHIP PUBLICATIONS
Greenville, Ohio

The Case of the Six Bullets, by R. M. Laurenson
© 2023 Coachwhip Publications edition

Cover: Todd A. Croteau / Library of Congress

First published 1949
Robert M. Laurenson, 1906-1982
CoachwhipBooks.com

ISBN 1-61646-571-9
ISBN-13 978-1-61646-571-1

1

Nora's eyes sparkled. "Wasn't the church beautiful, Marc?"

"Huh? Oh, sure."

"Such enthusiasm! Don't you like weddings?"

"Sometimes."

"Please, dear! Don't talk me to death."

Marc took his eyes from the road long enough to glance quickly at the pert girl beside him.

"Nora, what was wrong with the rehearsal this afternoon?"

"Wrong? Darling, nothing. Not a thing. Dolly was radiant and Karl so handsome. The church decorations were wonderful. Don't you think Janey, Miriam and I'll make attractive bridesmaids?" Slyly, Nora peeked at him.

"You will, anyway." He grinned at her. "But something's wrong. I had a feeling—" He shook his head. "What does Dolly's father think of it?"

"Mr. Porter? Pumping me about my boss, huh? He's pleased. He stopped in the middle of dictation this morning and muttered to himself. Guessed he'd make Karl vice-president."

"Karl's already factory sales manager. Rising fast, that boy! Wonder if that had anything to do with his fast switch from Miriam to Dolly?"

"Marc! You suspicious worm!"

"An ambitious lad, Karl."

"But Mr. Porter wouldn't be *that* partial to Dolly. He thinks as much of Miriam, even if she is Cynthia's daughter and not his own. He wouldn't care which one Karl married."

"Maybe. Cynthia *was* touchy."

Nora nodded. "Cynthia's different. But she doesn't appoint vice-presidents."

"How many're to be at dinner tonight?"

"The whole gang. Let's see." Nora counted on her fingers. "You and I, Mr. Porter and Cynthia, Dolly and Karl. That's six. Tony and Miriam—"

"That good-for-nothing roommate of mine coming? He didn't tell me."

"Miriam asked him this afternoon. Jane's coming with Ted Arthur, Joel and Mr. Porter's sister. Twelve."

"Good old Aunt Sarah! She'll pep up the party."

"Oh, Sarah's all right. Just a little touched with religion."

"And son Joel's just touched, eh?"

"You are cynical."

"Yes. Well, here we are."

Marc turned the gray Ford into a driveway, and stopped behind a row of cars. They crossed a wide, carefully tended lawn and mounted veranda steps. A butler swung open the door.

"Evening, Harrison." Marc solemnly gave the butler his hat and a slow wink.

"Good evening, sir. Miss O'Conner."

Marc stood in the door to the luxurious living room. Swiftly, his eyes scanned the occupants, pausing for an instant on each.

Porter leaned against the mantel, a powerful finger gripping a cigar like a billiard cue. His heavy features showed a trace of arrogance.

Near him, slender and vivacious, sat his wife Cynthia. Her flashing eyes darted to the newcomers.

Hands clasped, absorbed in a world of their own, Karl Snyder and Dolly perched on a davenport.

In a far corner, his pasty face puckered in concentration, Neal, the Porter heir apparent, thumbed a paperbound novel. Beside him his Aunt Sarah knitted and rocked, very fast.

A young man bounded to his feet and strode across the room. Seizing Marc's hand, he pumped it vigorously.

"Mr. Jordan! Delighted! An honor to have the eminent railroad attorney with us."

"Likewise the eminent Doctor Bodine!" replied Marc dryly. "Doctor, lawyer, merchant—who's the thief?"

"Don't carry your morbid curiosity too far, my lad. Miss O'Conner, come." With elaborate courtesy, Tony led Nora to a chair beside Miriam. "Miss Porter, Miss O'Conner. You should know each other."

Nora patted Miriam's knee affectionately. "Hi, Miriam. Haven't seen you for almost an hour!" She turned to Cynthia. "Are we last? I'm terribly embarrassed."

Cynthia smiled and shook her head. "No. Ted Arthur and Jane aren't here yet. You aren't late anyway."

Harrison again stepped to the door as she spoke and admitted the last of the guests, Ted and Jane. Fascinated, Marc's eyes followed them. The contrast between the two was startling. Jane, a lively, chuckling blonde, dropped to the davenport beside Dolly and hugged her excitedly.

"Oh, Dolly, it was fun," she said. "Your wedding will be lovely."

"Thanks, Jane," replied Dolly. "I hope so."

Somber and aloof, Ted, chemical engineer for Porter's brass company, stood just inside the door. His black eyes never left Dolly, and his face was strained. He tugged at his collar which seemed to choke him.

"Beg pardon, Mrs. Porter. Dinner is served."

Rigid, Harrison stood in the door and stared at a mantel clock. A chatter of gastronomic anticipation filled the room.

"Thank you, Harrison." Cynthia rose gracefully and slipped her hand under Porter's elbow. "Let's let Dolly and Karl go first, Don," she continued. "They've rehearsed the wedding; they might as well practice being hosts, too."

Porter smiled tolerantly at his wife.

"Call your shots, Cynthia. You're boss."

She turned to the radiant couple.

"Mrs. Snyder—oh—what rotten luck, Dolly! I shouldn't call you that before the wedding. But you'll have to get used to being married folks. You and Karl lead the way."

One bound, and Tony, his face a mixture of angelic boyishness and maturity, crossed the room. With a flourish, he drew an imaginary line on the carpet with his toe.

"Line forms," he said cheerfully. "Step up, folks. First the stars. Us lesser fry'll fall in behind."

"All right, Doctor," said Karl, helping Dolly to her feet. "When the great Bodine prescribes, common people listen." He turned to Mrs. Porter. "Cynthia, you letting Tony dictate etiquette in the Porter house tonight?"

Cynthia smiled wryly. "Think I could stop him? I wouldn't try."

Tony bowed formally. "Mrs. P., your trust and confidence overwhelm me."

He gently pushed Dolly and Karl into position at the edge of the carpet.

"Cynthia, you and Don next." Cynthia and Porter lined up.

"Then Ted and Janey. Then Marc and Nora. Joel and Aunt Sarah. Miriam and I'll graciously hold down the rear. Forward, march!" he commanded as the procession formed. "Here comes the bride! Here comes the bride! Dum dum de-dum!"

Gaily they paraded into the dining room.

"You're mighty cheerful, Tony," Marc said as they crossed the hall.

"Why not? My handsome and clever rival—to wit, Mr. Karl Snyder—gets married tomorrow, and not to my girl. God bless him!" He squeezed Miriam's arm. "Such a charming couple, aren't they?"

Miriam flinched and paled. Tony, catching the pain in her eyes despite the flickering candlelight, leaned over her quickly.

"Sorry, darling," he murmured. "Very thoughtless of me."

She gave him a wan smile. "Okay, Doc. Operation successful, even if the patient dies!"

Cynthia took her place at the head of the table. Seemingly tall, with a height born of poise and confidence rather than inches, she graciously waited for the others. She indicated the place at her right.

"Karl, the bridegroom on my right, please. Dolly next, if she can stand to be that far away! Marc—Nora—Joel." She touched the chair to her left and turned to her daughter. Her eyes softened. "Miriam, you, dear, then Tony, Jane, Ted and Aunt Sarah. All right, Harrison." She nodded to the butler.

They were all seated, except Porter. He tapped a knife against his plate, lifted a wine glass level with his eyes and admired the amber fluid.

"A toast! Dolly, I hope you make your sales manager husband so happy that he doubles our business next year!"

Karl grinned and slipped his hand through the crook of Dolly's arm. "With this inspiration, Don, I'll have your darn factory running on triple shifts. You'll have brass fittings coming out of your ears."

Glasses were raised, save by Joel, to Porter's left, and Sarah to his right. Joel's glass was long since empty. He crooked a finger at Harrison and pointed to it.

No wine glass stood before Sarah. From the sniffy angle of her nose it was plain that alcohol, even the mildest, never had, nor would, pass her lips. A tight white lace collar crowded her chin. Gray-black hair, tightly braided, was coiled on the top of her head like a snake, and pince-nez glasses rode the bridge of her nose. She stared down at Dolly.

"I hope your marriage lasts, Dorothy. 'Whom God hath brought together, let no man tear asunder.'"

Karl grinned at her. "Aunt Sarah, we're not married yet. Don't try to stir up trouble already."

"Humph. The Porter name's been unbesmirched. I fear for it."

Dolly's face flushed. She leaned forward and shook a finger at Joel.

"How about brother Joel? He's no angel. He's done quite a job of besmirching already!"

Sarah bristled. "Joel's misunderstood. You all pick on him."

Porter leaned over to his sister. "Sarah, hold your tongue."

Joel twirled his glass, emptied it, and signaled Harrison again.

"Folks," said Marc, rising, "I too propose a toast. To a cracking good salesman, a right guy, and his blushing bride. I hope their happiness starts tomorrow and lasts and lasts! And I'm going to kiss the bride good!"

"Marc!"

"You, too, darling," he said hastily, patting Nora's shoulder, "but with Dolly the chance only comes once."

"Hey," exclaimed Tony. "Chitchat. This lovely shrimp's getting old. I'm hungry."

Cynthia picked up her fork and smiled at him.

"All right, Doctor Bodine. We can't allow medicine's gift to the neurotic ladies of Calumet to suffer starvation."

"Thanks, Cynthia." Tony leaned close to Miriam and whispered in her ear. "Cheer up, Mimi. Karl's a heel. Forget him."

Miriam frowned. "That's the wrong approach, Tony."

"Come to my office after the wedding. I'll tell you exactly why I'm the guy you're meant to marry."

"I'm all right, but you'd better work on Ted! He's the type to blow his top."

Tony glanced at Ted who, rigid and morose, gnawed his mustache and stared at Dolly.

"By golly, you might be right!"

Nora toyed with her cocktail. Delicious, if one liked shrimp. She didn't. It made her sick. Her eyes roved over the table, took in the sparkling glass and silver twinkling in the candlelight. One by one, she studied her friends. Cynthia, the perfect hostess; her demure daughter Miriam; Porter's daughter Dolly. So different. Both attractive. But where Dolly was selfish, Miriam was generous; where Dolly was hard, Miriam was gentle. She loved them both.

And Jane Thompson, the fourth member of their childhood quartette. The happy-go-lucky spark plug of much of their youthful deviltry. She hoped Ted and Jane would hit it off.

Poor Ted! Silent, introverted, scientific. Dolly's sudden announcement had stabbed him to the heart. She shuddered. A strange gathering, seething below the surface. Tragic that hearts couldn't be controlled.

She peeked at Joel, who sat silent beside her and emptied his wine glass again and again. He was half-brother to Miriam and Dolly, yet cut from different cloth. Then her eyes traveled across the table to Joel's Aunt Sarah. Sarah nibbled her shrimp, scarcely opening her mouth. Nora wondered vaguely whether she had teeth; her lips seldom opened far enough to tell. Sarah was Joel's champion.

Harrison whisked away the cocktail dishes, as skillfully served heaping dinner plates. Nora pressed her shoulder against Marc.

"Mr. Jordan, yoo-hoo! Remember me?"

He turned to her, a grin stretching the corners of his wide mouth. "Beg pardon? Oh, Miss O'Conner. Glad to see you. How've you been?"

"The fickleness of man!"

Marc turned to Porter. "Don, how's your new secretary? Have any trouble with her?"

Porter chuckled. "Shouldn't say it in her hearing, Marc, but she's wonderful. How'd you happen to let her get away from the railroad office?"

"Let me?" Nora snorted. "They couldn't keep me. I heard railroads all day at work, and all evening from Marc or Dad. That's the trouble with having a father and a boy friend working for a railroad. Besides, your salary scale's more attractive."

"You'll probably have to beat her about once a week," said Marc. "Anyway, I miss her."

"The enchantment of distance, dear."

"Dad," Dolly leaned forward, "my birthday's only a month away. How about advancing my present?"

"Why, you mercenary little witch!" growled Porter. "A thousand dollars, huh? Ain't your new car enough?"

Dolly pouted. "It's lovely, but think of the things we'll have to buy. Furniture. Drapes. An awning for our terrace."

"You've hoarded your birthday checks for years. Use some of that."

"Oh, no, Dad. That's all invested."

"I'll be darned. My own daughter. Tighter'n a tick on a dog! Borrow some from Miriam."

"I tried." Dolly frowned at Miriam. "She's tight, too. Says she's broke."

"Broke?" exclaimed Porter. "Why, she's—"

Cynthia choked violently. Clutching her napkin to her face, she escaped into the pantry. Miriam jumped up to help her mother, and several others moved to follow.

"Sit still," said Porter. "She'll be okay. Does that all the time."

In a few minutes Cynthia returned, touching a hand-kerchief to her bloodshot eyes.

"I'm terribly sorry," she apologized. "Some coffee went down the wrong way."

"Drink it, Ma," muttered Joel. "Don't breathe it."

"Do you good, young man," said Porter severely, "to breathe more and drink less."

"Donald, leave the boy alone!" Sarah glared at her brother through her bifocals. "He's high-strung."

"High-strung!" Dolly spit the words out. "He should be whipped!"

"Listen, you—!" Joel shoved his chair back and started to his feet. His father laid a restraining hand on his arm.

"Sit down, Joel," he snapped.

Miriam leaned forward, her face pale. "Dad! Dolly! Joel! Behave."

Marc caught Tony's eye as he took in the outburst with professional interest. Cynthia broke the embarrassed silence that followed by signaling Harrison to clear the table.

Tony turned to Miriam. "At this point, Miriam, how about a harmonica solo?"

"All right, laugh. But I like to play the harmonica."

"Sure. That's what I said. I love to hear you."

"She's got a new one, with a lever," said Joel. "Plays half-tones. Boy, does she stink!"

"Speaking of her music, I presume," said Marc dryly.

"Can you play a harmonica?" demanded Miriam. "Can you play anything but gin rummy?"

"Miriam," said Cynthia quietly, "not you too."

"Sorry, Mother."

"Who's laughing?" asked Jane. "Look at Larry Adler. Miriam's going to be an artist and make us all famous."

"Thanks, Janey," replied Miriam. "Now tell them about yourself."

"Secrets, Jane?" asked Ted, a shadow of a smile twitching the corners of his mouth.

"She's a harmonica virtuoso, too."

Nora chuckled. "Jane, you never mentioned it!"

Jane shook her blonde curls. "Please, folks, don't urge me. I won't play! I tried Miriam's one day, and it's fun! I can play *Dixie.*"

"Speaking of playing, Ted," said Marc, "how's your chess game? Taken on Oscar Witherspoon lately?"

Ted shook his head. "No. Haven't had time."

"Ted's too busy working on his new formula, God bless him. How's it, Ted?"

"Hard to tell, Mr. Porter. Looks hopeful."

"What're you working on, Ted?" asked Cynthia.

"A copper alloy. If it works, Mr. Porter should be able to charge more for a better—and cheaper—valve."

"That's what I like." Porter thumped the table with his fist. "That's my chemist. You dream up the stuff, Ted. I'll make it, Karl'll sell it. Mebbe I should take you birds in as partners."

"It's easier for a camel to pass through the eye of a needle than for a rich man to enter the Kingdom of God," quoted Sarah in a low, brittle voice.

Ted stared at his plate. Slowly his glittering eyes turned to Karl.

"No thanks!" he said softly.

"Sarah, you sanctimonious—!"

"Don!" Cynthia's voice cracked like a shot.

"Okay. But I'm not that rich. And don't I help support St. Luke's?"

"With your money. Not your heart." Sarah's lip barely moved.

Marc's eyes again met Tony's. A buzz of conversation covered the strain.

"Karl, where're you taking Dolly for a honeymoon?" asked Jane. "You've never told us."

"And I won't. You're too anxious."

"None of your business, Janey," said Dolly impudently. "That's between us." She patted Karl's hand.

"Are you driving Dolly's new car?" asked Tony.

"That," replied Karl, "is a leading question. And also none of your business."

"I was just curious."

"Uh-huh. Ideas like stones in the gas tanks or soap signs on the windows never entered your head, did they?"

"No." Tony smiled at him angelically.

"I hope the wedding goes as well as the rehearsal this afternoon. It was lovely," said Nora.

"Were you nervous, Karl?" asked Marc. "You didn't show it."

"A few extra palpitations. Dolly's the cucumber. She'll pull me through." He slid his arm across Dolly's shoulder and planted a kiss squarely on her lips.

Ted winced as though flicked with a whip.

Harrison, entering with a tray of coffee cups, stopped behind Cynthia and stared down aghast. The beautiful head of a tawny, gold and white collie lay in Miriam's lap. Soft brown eyes rolled from Miriam's face to the butler in supplication.

Miriam chuckled. "Rags wants to join the party."

Harrison bent over Cynthia's shoulder. "Sorry, Madam. He must've slipped by me."

"Never mind, Harrison. He's all right."

"You don't want to miss the fun, do you, boy?" Miriam fondled the soft ears. "Here you are." She selected a chocolate cream from a dish on the table and popped it into his mouth. "Now, lie down, Rags. Lie down."

"I can't get over Rags' love of candy," said Nora.

"Not candy," laughed Miriam; "chocolate creams. Very special chocolate creams. He's choosy. Takes the offer of anything else as an insult to his good taste."

"I knew a dog once that'd howl its head off when his mistress played one particular number on the piano," said Tony. "No other music bothered him. Crazy things, dogs. Almost human."

"You probe into too many neurotics, Tony," said Ted. "It dims your perspective."

"Folks," said Porter, draining his coffee cup, "I've reserved a table at the Ship's Hold. How about it? Wanta move down there? You youngsters can dance; Cynthia and I'll enjoy the floor show."

"All of us?" asked Jane.

"Sure. All that want to."

Cynthia pressed her hand to her forehead. "I don't believe I'll go, Don. I've a headache. This's been a busy day and tomorrow will be worse. You take the children."

"I think it'd be fun," said Dolly.

"Me too," agreed Nora. "The Ship's Hold! Marc never takes me there."

"At a ten-dollar cover charge? You gold-digger." Nora made a face at him.

"Count me out, Pop," said Joel.

"What're you up to?" demanded Porter.

"Oh," Joel blew smoke rings at the ceiling, "I'm working on an angle."

"Watch your step, you young whipper snapper. You get in a jam and you'll stay there."

"I'm taking precautions, Pop."

"Well, let's go. How about transportation? Everyone a way of getting there?"

"Transportation," chuckled Tony, "is something we've got. This's the car-iest family in Calumet!"

In a scurry of confusion, the party gathered up wraps and collected on the lawn.

The house was long and low, set on a corner some distance from the street in a beautifully landscaped grove. The side street was to the left, at a level slightly higher than the lawn. A flagstone walk led from the veranda steps to an opening in the hedge.

To the right a three-car garage stood a few feet from the end of the house, approached by a white graveled drive. Cars were lined up in the driveway. Porter's big limousine stood inside the open door. Behind it was parked Dolly's shiny new sedan. Tony's coupé—his "dollbuggy"—with Marc's weather-beaten gray Ford nudging its bumper came next. Ted Arthur's car brought up the rear.

The couples fanned out to their respective vehicles. Tony waved his hand at the line.

"See what I mean? Cars'n cars. Some little blue flags, and we'd make a fine funeral procession. Hey! That's an idea. Let's have a parade."

"I'll have to parade to a gas station first, Tony. I'm about out."

"You need gas, Marc?" called Porter. "I'll fix you up. Come here."

Porter snapped on the light in the garage and led the way to the back where a big tank stood on a stand. He selected a can from several on a low steel rack below the tank. Twisting the spigot, he started to fill the can.

Marc followed him into the garage. "Never mind, Don," he protested. "I'll stop at a gas station."

"No bother, Marc." Porter waved at the tank. "Got better'n two hundred gallons here. Be glad to get rid of it."

Marc filled a second can and returned to his car with Porter. As they came around the end of the car, they found

Ted staring morosely into his, and Jane clutching his arm, convulsed with laughter. Nora stood beside them.

"What's so funny?" asked Marc.

"Ted locked his car—with the keys inside," replied Nora.

"Afraid someone'd steal that pile of junk?"

"What's the delay?" asked Tony, joining the group. "Locked out, Ted? A fine thing. You've got us all plugged in. Now what do we do?"

"Ted locks his car when he stops to mail a letter," chuckled Jane. "He's a pessimist."

"Okay, I'm dumb," replied Ted ruefully. "Habit, I guess. Think I can get in. This's happened before. Do you have a big screwdriver, Don, and a flashlight?"

Porter went back into the garage and returned with a bag of tools and a flashlight. Ted opened the trunk, removed four screws that held the back set and pushed it into the car. Crawling through the opening, he emerged in a moment grinning and triumphant.

"Nothing to it," he said. "Had to do that one night on Main Street, then argue with a cop about stealing my own car!"

"All right, move that animated tin can," said Tony. "Let's go dance."

Finally the procession got under way. Nora snuggled against Marc's shoulder.

"I like the Porters, but it's nice to be alone for a minute," she said.

Marc smiled at her. "That's right. They're a strenuous family."

"I thought Mr. Porter was going to snap Joel's head off."

"The old man's mad because he got booted out of college."

"What happened?"

Marc shrugged. "Don't know exactly. Something about some girls and a wild party."

"I hope he doesn't get into serious trouble. It'd be terrible for the family."

"I feel sorry for Ted. Poor guy. He looked like he was being crucified."

Nora shot a sidewise glance at him. "He is. Didn't you know?"

"In a way, yes. But I didn't think he'd take it so hard."

"He adores Dolly. He told me she was the only girl he ever loved. Why do people tell *me* their troubles?"

"Because you're such a sweet, soft-hearted listener."

"And Miriam. Why couldn't those four have paired off the other way?"

"That question's been popping up for thousands of years. Even Psychiatrist Bodine doesn't know the answer. Tony's happy about the whole thing. Gives him a chance with Miriam."

"I hope so. Tony's nice, if he is a doctor!"

They drove in silence for several blocks. Nora slid her hand under Marc's elbow.

"Are you going to stand me up some day, Marc?"

He squeezed her hand. "Not a chance. I like your eyes, your funny nose, and you!"

She laid her head on his shoulder. "Um-mm. I'm glad."

Marc and Nora were the first to arrive at the Ship's Hold. It reeked with atmosphere. The entrance led over a swaying gangplank. Artificial wind flapped the canvas shroud and whistled through cracks. The gangplank ended in a pilot house. A man in natty nautical attire slowly turned a big wheel and stared intently into a night scene painted on the wall.

Behind him, steps led down to the "deck," which was filled with tables, except for a tiny dance floor in the center. At the far end of the deck, a bar was set into a bulkhead and above the bar a dance band crooned softly. Life preservers were hung at strategic points, in case of emergency.

A headwaiter bounded up the steps to the pilot house at the sight of Mr. Porter.

"Good evening, sir," he said. "Glad to see you. Come this way, please. I've a good table for your party."

He led the way to a long table at one side of the deck.

"Be amusing, Marc," said Nora. "Don't let me look at the walls. I get seasick!" She pointed to the walls. A rail formed each side of the deck. A few feet beyond the rails, sea scenes slowly moved up and down, giving an eerie sense of a slowly rolling ship.

Marc chuckled. "Bad psychology, I think. Makes a fellow think he's drunk before he is!"

"There aren't many here yet, Marc. Let's dance before the place gets jammed."

"A fine idea."

They whirled away on the almost deserted floor. Before the number was over, they were joined by Tony and Miriam.

"See you made it," called Marc. "I wouldn't bet on your getting home, though. Watch him, Miriam."

"Just mind your own intake, son. Bodine can take it."

At the end of the dance they rejoined Porter, who sat in solitary splendor. At that moment Ted and Jane arrived.

Porter waved to a waiter. "What'll it be, folks? Jane?"

"Martini, please."

"Ted?"

"Double Scotch and soda."

"Miriam?"

She shook her head. "Not just yet, Dad."

"Tony?"

"Double Scotch. No soda."

Miriam gasped. "Tony!"

He slid his hand along the back of her chair. "This's a party. Remember? I'm celebrating."

"Go to it, Tony," chuckled Porter. "Marc?"

"Beer."

"Nora?"

"A Daiquiri, please."

"Hey!" Marc glared at her. "Where'd you get such fancy ideas?"

Nora gently twisted his nose between her thumb and forefinger. "A party, darling. Remember?"

"Don't get the habit. My salary doesn't run so high."

"Here comes the bride! All fat and wide!" Tony pounded the table and stamped his feet on the floor.

Dolly, pale and subdued, was guided to the table by a grinning Karl.

"I wonder," continued Tony thoughtfully, "what delayed them. Any ideas?"

Karl thumbed his nose at him. "Do your mind reading during office hours, Doc."

"How about a drink, kids?" asked Porter. "What'll you have, Doll?"

She shook her head. "Nothing, thanks. I don't feel very well."

The music blared out with a crash. As one, the four couples headed for the dance floor.

"Okay, sweet," said Karl. "Let's dance now, drink later."

The drinks were served by the time they all got back to the table. Porter scowled at them.

"A fine bunch of kids! Go off and leave me alone."

Miriam patted his hand. "Sorry, Dad. It's a shame Mother couldn't come, so you could have fun too."

"Okay, okay. Well, tomorrow's the day, hey?" Porter put his arm around Dolly and squeezed her. "I lose a daughter and gain a son."

Karl laughed. "I'm worried. What'll I call you tomorrow? Pop? Dad? Don? Or sir?"

"Just stick to Boss, my boy. And don't get any ideas about a soft job."

"Dolly, how many kids are you going to have?" demanded Jane.

"Jane!" Tony stared at her in astonishment. "Come to my office in the morning. I want to have a talk with you!"

Ted's face turned ashen. He drained his glass and waved to the waiter for a refill.

Two spots formed in Dolly's pale cheeks. "Janey," she said softly, "you'll have to wait and see."

"I'm sorry, Dolly," replied Jane.

Marc caught Miriam watching him intently. She moved her head almost imperceptibly toward the dance floor.

"Miriam," he said, "will you dance with me?"

"Surely, Marc," she replied, rising quickly.

"Hey! Stealing my girl, huh?" Tony leaped to his feet. "No roommate o' mine can get away with that. I'll steal yours. Come on, Irish."

Marc and Miriam circled the floor in silence. Then he looked down at her.

"You're lovely tonight, Miriam. You put the bride to shame."

"Karl doesn't think so," she murmured.

"He's a fool. I'm tempted to make a pass at you myself. I could run that flea-brained friend of mine right out of town."

"And break Nora's heart? You couldn't, Marc."

"No, that's right, I couldn't," he said softly.

"Marc—" Miriam hesitated. "I'm worried."

"I thought so. What is it, Miriam?"

"I don't know exactly. Have you noticed how jumpy Dolly is?"

"She does seem off her feed. I charged it to prewedding jitters."

"It's very unusual. Dolly's usually cool and collected, and Mother too."

"Your mother?"

"Yes. She was upset at dinner. She was looking forward to this party. She suggested it, in fact."

"I don't see what there is to be worried about. A wedding's quite a strain, I'm told, on both Mama and daughter."

"Yes, but—" Miriam hesitated again. She looked up at him, her eyes misty. "Maybe I'm silly, Marc. But I stumbled onto an argument between Mother and Dolly this afternoon. They were in the den. I went in there for something and surprised them."

Marc pressed her gently. "Miriam, my girl, you are silly. Everyone has arguments. Probably about some detail of the wedding."

She shook her head. "No. They froze up when I came in. Wouldn't explain a thing."

"What were they talking about?"

"Something about 'that man.' I didn't hear much."

"What man could it be?"

"I don't know. A tramp came to the door this morning, but they wouldn't squabble about that."

"Doesn't Cynthia approve of Karl?"

"Oh, yes! At least, I never heard her say anything against him."

"Then if I were you, I'd forget it. It's probably some little thing that doesn't matter."

"Thanks, Marc." She smiled at him. "I knew you'd cheer me up."

"And another thing—you won't brush off our friend, Doctor Bodine? He's a darn nice guy, you know, if he is a little light-headed."

"I know. I like Tony very much."

They strolled back to the table, threading their way through the growing crowd. Porter had the waiter at his elbow, renewing the drink orders. Dolly pressed fingertips to her temples and shook her head.

"Nothing for me, Dad." She turned to Karl. "I'd like to go home, Karl. Will you take me, please?"

"Home? Dolly, it's early."

Porter pulled out his watch. "It's only ten-thirty!"

"I know, but I've a headache. You stay. Will you take me, Karl?"

"Sure," he said, helping her with her coat. Together they climbed the steps to the pilot house and disappeared up the gangplank. Ted's eyes followed them as he drained his glass.

There was a crash from the orchestra, the lights dimmed and a spotlight shone on the dance floor. A lithe couple whirled into the gyrations of an adagio dance.

When the lights came up at the end of the number, Marc turned to the table for his matches. Ted was helping Jane with her coat.

"I'd better go too," he said. "Good night, Don. Thanks for the party."

"Okay, Ted. Glad to have you. Better stay, though. There's a good show."

Ted shook his head. "Have to check a heat test at the lab. See you tomorrow."

They followed Karl and Dolly.

At the end of the show, Nora turned to Marc. "Maybe we'd better go too, Marc."

"Yes," said Miriam. "Tomorrow's a big day."

"What's the matter with you kids? Can't take it, huh?"

"That's right, Don. Been a nice party," said Tony.

"All right, beat it. I'll see the man about the check and have another beer."

"Not too many, Don," said Marc, "and keep your eyes off that blonde!"

Porter chuckled. "No danger, my boy. Not here!"

They negotiated the swaying gangplank and stepped into the cool night. Nora breathed deeply.

"Um-mm. Fresh air smells good!"

"So long, folks," called Marc. "Tony, hurry home. None of this all-night stuff."

Tony made a circle with his thumb and forefinger.

"'Bye, Jordan. Nice knowing you."

Marc helped Nora into the car. She stretched out and leaned her head against the cushion.

"Hungry?"

She shook her head. "No. Tired. Let's go home, Marc."

He nodded and headed the Ford into the night owl traffic. Leaving the night life district, he drove for ten minutes through quiet residential streets, finally stopped before a modest brick house.

He slid his arm around Nora's shoulders, pulled her to him and kissed her gently. She snuggled into the crook of his arm. They sat thus for several minutes. Then Nora stirred, and brushed her lips across Marc's cheek.

"Good night, Marc. I must go."

"Good night, Irish," he said, pressing her to him. "See you tomorrow."

He accompanied her to the door and returned, lighting a chipped black briar pipe.

A train whistle, muted by distance, echoed along the quiet street. Marc glanced at his watch.

"Overland Flier," he muttered. "Right on time."

With a clash of gears, he pulled away from the curb and headed into the night.

2

Marc had scarcely settled himself in bed with a book, the radio going and Tillie cuddled beside him, when the door popped open.

Tony sniffed. "Wow! Tillie's sand box needs an airing!"

Marc grinned at him. "Sure your nose isn't twisted?"

"Cats! I'm tempted to kick that feline fuzz ball right out of here."

Marc fondled the soft ears, to Tillie's purring delight. "Mathilde, our friend's being nasty."

The telephone rang, and Marc reached for it.

"Jordan speaking."

"Hello, Marc. O'Conner. Baxter called a little bit ago. He's hoggin' the Overland. He hit a car at Elm Way crossing."

"Elm Way—that's just a back road. Anyone hurt?"

"Dunno. Baxter run by a quarter-mile, an' called before he had time to check up."

"Did he tell you any more about it?"

"Not much. Bad curve there. Says he just gotta flash of the car standin' on the crossin' before he hit. You'll have damages to worry about. I figgered you'd wanta to check on it."

"That's right, Johnny. I'll go right out."

"Let me know what the score is."

"I'll call you. Did you notify the police?"

"Not yet, but I will."

"Okay, John. Thanks."

Marc returned the telephone to its cradle and hopped out of bed, dumping Tillie unceremoniously to the floor. Quickly he started dressing.

"What's up?" asked Tony. "Our eminent chief attorney get a hurry call?"

"Wreck. The Overland hit a car at Elm Way. I'll have to find out about it."

"Hm. Trouble, trouble, trouble. Glad I'm a doctor and not a railroader."

"After that crack, how about coming along?"

Tony thought a moment. "Why not? Might be some interesting psychological reactions to observe."

"You cold-blooded fish! Psychological reactions!"

"How about you? All you'll think about is how to keep the damages down."

"Come on; let's go."

They hurried to the basement garage and climbed into Marc's car. Skillfully he worked it out of the garage and headed toward town.

"Elm Way," he said thoughtfully. "That's not so far from Porter's. If I remember right, it turns off their street out about eight or ten blocks, and cuts through the woods."

"Don't kid me, Jordan. That's Petter's Paradise! You know it as well as I do."

Marc laughed softly. "Not lately. O'Conner's porch is more convenient! Enjoy the party tonight?"

"Yes and no. Miriam wasn't much fun. Sort of touchy. I sure like that little gal."

"Take it easy, Tony."

He nodded. "Yeah."

They drove in silence through the dark streets. As Marc slowed to turn into Elm Way, a car approached from the opposite direction and turned in. A police car. Marc followed along the narrow, winding dirt road. Halfway down a gentle grade, the police car stopped short of the railroad crossing. Marc parked in back of it, fished a powerful flashlight out of the glove compartment, and slid from behind the wheel. He joined a lanky officer who climbed out of the police car.

"Hello, Pete," he said.

"Howdy, Mr. Jordan. What's cookin'?"

"You know as much as I do. Let's go and see."

They walked to the crossing where flickering light from flashlights and lanterns dimly illuminated a milling knot of people. Marc, Tony, and Pete followed the track for twenty feet or so to where a trainman stood with a lantern.

"Hello, Holland," said Marc. "A little trouble?"

"Howdy, Mr. Jordan." Holland's face was pale and grim. He pointed to the torn, mangled, blood-splattered body of a man lying beside the track. The upper part of what was left of him hung over the embankment. "What d'you think?"

Marc's stomach turned over as he looked at the bundle of rags and flesh.

"What a mess! Who is it?"

"Dunno," said Holland. "We didn't wanta touch anything until the police got here."

Pete leaned over the man and fished through his pockets. "This's one job I sure hate," he said.

Marc climbed down the low bank and flashed his light into the man's face. A horrified gasp escaped him.

"It's Ted!" he exclaimed. "Ted Arthur!"

"Judas!" said Tony. He leaped down beside Marc. "I'll be hanged if it isn't."

They looked at each other in stunned silence for several minutes. Marc turned back to Holland.

"Anyone else?" he asked.

"There's a girl in the car," he said. "Dead." He pointed fifty feet farther along the track to where a twisted, tangled mass of steel lay in the ditch. Tony dashed to the car, his nonchalance gone, and an agony of apprehension contorting his face. Marc followed close on his heels. He played his light around and into the wreck.

The shoulders and head of a girl, clad in a dainty, blood-soaked white dress, were crushed between the seat and steering wheel. Her forehead rested on the rim of the wheel, and the rest of her body was hidden by the crumpled wreckage.

A dry sob whistled through Tony's lips. Trembling, he gripped the side of the car for support. His tortured eyes turned to Marc.

"Dolly!" he whispered. "My God, poor Dolly! I was afraid—"

Marc nodded shakily. He turned away and stared into the woods for several minutes. Regaining control of himself, he walked over to the officer.

"Pete," he said, "how'd you like to handle this?"

"I'll send Jake back for the coroner. We'll have to keep this gang of people away till he gets here."

"I'd like to take some pictures. That be all right with you?"

"Sure. Go ahead."

"Most of these people're passengers, aren't they, Holland?"

"That's right."

"Get 'em back on the train. How's the engine? Any damage?"

"Don't think so. Baxter's checking it now."

"If you can move, take your train into Calumet. When you call O'Conner, tell him to get the section gang out to check this track. I want to see you and the rest of the crew tomorrow."

"Yes, sir. All right, folks. Everybody on board. We leave in five minutes."

Reluctantly, the morbidly curious group of staring people straggled back to the train, the rear of which was out of sight several hundred feet down the track.

Marc walked to his car to get his photographic equipment. He played his light along the side of the road. He glanced at tracks in the shallow ditch opposite the two parked cars: the tracks of the left wheel of a car that had stopped short of the crossing, and backed away. Footprints led to the crossing and back.

By the time he located his box of equipment and returned to the wreck, most of the onlookers had drifted back to the train. He rigged his camera with a flash bulb attachment and photographed Ted's body from several angles. Then he did the same with the car. He had difficulty finding a position that would include the limp body of Dolly, but he took a number of shots and hoped for the best.

A half hour was consumed. The train moved on, leaving the three men to guard the gruesome spot.

No word was spoken. Pete stood beside the car, and Tony paced back and forth along the track, chain-smoking cigarettes.

Marc returned to his car with the camera. On an impulse, he stopped at the marks in the mud and snapped a picture. He was stowing his equipment in the back seat when a cavalcade of autos pulled up: the police car; an ambulance; a garage wrecking car.

The Calumet county coroner led the procession that climbed out of the cars.

"Well, Jordan," he called, "got some corpses, eh?"

Marc nodded. "Afraid so, Doc."

The coroner walked to where Pete stood over Ted's body. He glanced at it quickly. Then he went to the car and repeated his cursory examination.

"Death by accident," he said. "Take 'em away, boys."

Two men with a stretcher gathered up Ted and slid his mortal remains into the ambulance. Dolly was another matter. Using crowbars and hack saws, they worked for an hour before her crumpled body could be freed.

In the meantime Marc joined Tony.

"We've done all we can, Tony, except"—he hesitated —"tell the Porter family."

Tony nodded. "Been thinking about that. How I dread it!"

"So do I. But it's got to be done. Let's get it over with."

He walked to the men working on the car.

"We're leaving, Doc. I'll stop at Porter's and break the news."

"Okay, Jordan. We'll handle this."

Silently they drove to the Porter house. A light in the garage showed through the open door to one of the stalls. Lights burned in the living room, and in a second floor bedroom. As they mounted the steps to the veranda, they could see Miriam sitting in a corner of the davenport reading. Marc pressed the bell button.

In a few seconds the veranda was flooded with light, and Miriam stood in the door, her eyebrows arched in surprise.

"Marc and Tony!" she exclaimed. "What on earth—?"

"May we come in?" asked Marc.

"Of course. But isn't it a little late for a call?"

"Ordinarily, yes. Where're the rest of the family?"

"Mother and Dad have gone to bed. Joel is out, and so's Dolly. She hasn't come home from the party yet."

"I see." Marc hesitated. "Miriam, I'd like to talk to your father and mother. Would you call them, please?"

A puzzled frown creased her forehead. "But, Marc, I don't understand."

"Please, Miriam. It's quite important. I'll explain."

"Yes, Marc."

She disappeared up the stairs. Marc stepped to a cubbyhole under the stairs, consulted a telephone directory, and called a number.

"Hello, Karl; Marc Jordan. Will you come over to Porter's right away? . . . I know it, Karl; but something serious has just occurred. . . . Yes. Please hurry. It's very important."

He hung up and joined Tony in the living room.

"Don't think I can take it, Marc," muttered Tony.

"Brace up. Where's the nerve doctor's nerves?"

"Yeah, but this's different!"

Miriam returned, followed by Cynthia in an ankle-length house coat and Porter in slapping slippers, pajamas and bathrobe.

"What the dickens?" asked Porter in annoyance. "What deviltry're you birds up to?"

"Sorry, Don," replied Marc. "Can't be helped."

He packed his pipe with tobacco, slowly lit it.

"Have any of you seen Dolly since the party?"

Puzzled glances were exchanged. Porter shook his head. "No. She isn't home yet. She and Karl're out spooning."

Marc turned to Miriam. "Have you seen her?"

Miriam also shook her head. "No, Marc. Why do you ask?"

He sucked on his pipe for several minutes.

"This's one of the hardest things I've ever had to do," he said slowly. "Dolly must've come home from the party. Anyway, sometime after we last saw her at the Ship's Hold, she left Karl and went for a ride with Ted." He paused. "Dolly's car was struck by the Overland Flier at Elm Way. They were both killed!"

"Killed!" Porter gasped. His mouth sagged open, and the network of veins around his nose stood out like a map. "Did you say Dolly's been killed?"

Cynthia moaned softly, chewed at the knuckles of her clenched fist, swayed and tumbled in a heap on the floor.

Miriam, sobbing wildly, dropped to her knees beside her mother and cradled her head in her lap. Tony sprang to her side. Gently, he picked up Cynthia and laid her on the davenport.

Porter collapsed into a chair and clutched his head in his hands, moaning softly.

"Get some water, Marc," rasped Tony.

In clumsy haste Marc hurried to the kitchen. He snapped on the light and fumbled in the cupboard for a glass. His elbow struck a rolling pin which rolled across the table and clattered to the floor unheeded. He filled the glass and returned to the living room.

Cynthia was stretched out on the davenport. Tony had propped up her feet with cushions. Miriam, tears streaming down her cheeks, moistened her handkerchief and dabbed her mother's face. Cynthia stirred and her eyelids fluttered. She moaned, and struggled to sit up. Gently, Tony pushed her down.

"Easy, Cynthia," he said. "Lie still a minute."

Her breath came in great gasps. Slowly the color returned to her cheeks. She slid her feet to the floor, straightened up and dropped her head against the cushion.

"Poor Dolly," she whimpered.

Marc walked to Porter and laid a hand on his shoulder. "I'm sorry, Don."

Porter slowly looked up, his eyes glazed, his face haggard and pale.

"Dolly's dead! My baby's dead, mangled in a car!"

Marc gave his shoulder a sympathetic squeeze.

Miriam was the first to regain control of herself. She sat beside her mother and slid an arm around her waist. The other hand held a handkerchief to her lips.

"What was it, Marc?" she whispered. "What happened?"

Marc shrugged. "I don't know exactly. The facts are that Dolly's car was hit by the train, and Ted and she were both instantly killed. Unless someone in the house saw Dolly, I've no idea how she happened to be with Ted, and at the crossing. I've called Karl. He'll be here in a minute. Perhaps he knows something."

Cynthia heaved a great sigh. "I can't understand. What could Dolly have been thinking of, the night before her wedding?"

"Who knows? A last good-bye, perhaps."

The lights of a car swung into the drive. In a few seconds feet pounded on the veranda and Karl burst into the room. He was hatless and worried. His glance swept the room.

"What's up?" he demanded.

"Oh, Karl!" cried Miriam. Her eyes flooded with tears and she pressed her fingers to her cheeks.

"What is it?" he repeated. "My God, what's the matter with all of you?"

Marc laid his hand on Karl's shoulder.

"Karl," he said slowly, dragging the words out by sheer will power, "Dolly's had an accident."

"Accident? Is she hurt?"

"She's—" The words stalled on Marc's lips. "She's dead, Karl!"

A shuddering convulsion jerked Karl's body. He gripped Marc's arms and shook him violently.

"Damn you, Jordan, what are you saying?"

"Her car was struck by a train. She was killed instantly."

Cynthia ran unsteadily to Karl, threw her arms around his waist and buried her head on his coat, crying softly.

A spasm of bewildered horror swept Karl's face. "But I brought her home myself! She can't be—" He stopped and looked down at Cynthia. "I kissed her, right here, not an hour ago. She can't be dead. What is this frightful joke?"

"Sit down, Karl," said Marc. "Get a grip on yourself. Did you bring Dolly home?"

"Sure I did. Left her right here."

"Did she say anything about going out again?"

"Of course not. I put her car away, and came in with her. She said she'd take some Pepsin and go to bed so she'd feel well tomorrow. Tomorrow! Tomorrow was to be my wedding day." He looked at Marc in shocked surprise. "And now there won't be any wedding."

Porter rose slowly and walked to Karl. He put his hand on his arm for a moment, then went to a window and stared out.

Miriam dabbed at her eyes. "Ted was with her, Karl," she whispered. "He was killed too."

"Ted!" exclaimed Karl. "What was he doing with Dolly?"

"That's what we'd like to know," said Marc. "Sure she didn't act as though she had some reason for coming home early?"

Karl shook his head wearily. "No—no! She said she was going to bed."

Marc re-lit his dead pipe. He walked back to the kitchen and headed for the sink. His foot struck a man's shiny, freshly washed overshoe and he stooped to straighten it. He picked up a spoon lying on the drain board and sniffed it. Slowly he returned to the living room.

"I know the smell of Pepsin," he said. "Someone had a dose this evening. Wonder if anyone else saw Dolly? How about Joel, or Aunt Sarah, or the Harrisons?"

"The Harrisons went to bed long ago," said Cynthia. "So did Sarah, I believe. I thought I heard Joel come in, but his room's empty."

"Well," said Marc, "it's not important." He joined Porter at the window. "Sorry, Don. I'll have to see you in the morning about damages, and so forth. They're at the morgue, if you want to attend to things tonight."

Porter stared at him blankly, and nodded. A soft shriek came from Miriam. She tore the corner of her handkerchief with her teeth.

"Come on, Tony," said Marc roughly. "Let's go."

They left the room precipitately. At the door, Tony looked back at the forlorn group. Their departure had gone unnoticed.

Marc stopped on the step and glanced toward the side street. He followed the flagstone path to the sidewalk and turned his flashlight on a car parked at the curb. Ted Arthur's car. He opened the door and probed the interior with his light. It was clean and empty.

Completing his examination, he rejoined Tony who waited at the step.

"Now what?"

"Ted's car," replied Marc laconically.

They climbed into the Ford and backed out of the drive. Marc had to run over the lawn to get by Karl's car, but somehow he felt that Porter wouldn't care.

"What d'you make of it?" asked Tony.

"You can guess. Poor, heart-sick Ted saw Dolly come home. He dropped in, persuaded her to go for a ride. They were probably so intent on straightening out their heartaches they didn't see the train. Result—two bodies!"

They drove in silence for several blocks.

"You know, human beings are heels. Speaking of myself," Tony added hastily. "Know what I'm thinking about this horrible business? Selfishly, I'm afraid my chances with Miriam are shot!"

3

Marc pulled the car into the basement garage and turned off the ignition. He sat silent for a moment. Tony had started to climb out when he spoke suddenly.

"Wait a minute, Tony."

"Now what?"

"There's something strange about this. You think so?"

"No. Only thing strange is why you fellows don't have crossing lights."

"Not enough traffic. That isn't what I mean. Seems to me O'Conner said Dolly's car was standing at the crossing."

"What's funny about that?"

"On a crossing? Darn peculiar place to park!"

"So it is!"

"I'm going to call John and ask him."

He swung his legs out and mounted the steps three at a time. Entering the apartment, he went straight to the telephone and quickly dialed a number.

"Z.A. tower!"

"Hello, Johnny. Jordan. Did Holland call you?"

"Yeah. Train's okay and left town."

"When you called before, you said that Baxter told you the car was standing at the crossing. Did I hear right?"

"Yeah. That's right. Why?"

"I see. You're sure?"

"Sure I'm sure. Baxter's here now. Ask him yourself."

"Tell him to stay there. I want to talk to him."

"All right, Marc. Comin' now?"

"On my way."

He put down the telephone and started for the door.

"Coming, Tony?"

"Where?"

"Z.A. tower. I want to talk to the engine crew."

"Beds," said Tony, pointing to the twin beds, "are made to be used. Know what time it is?"

"Late. But I can't sleep. Neither will you. Come on. I'm not satisfied about this at all."

"I don't know which is worse, living with a railroader or being one! Good-bye sleep! Can't use you tonight!"

They hurried to the garage and again Marc drove out, returning to the business district. The streets were practically deserted and he tore along, disregarding possible traffic or traffic cops. He crossed to the far side of the city, followed a cinder road across a network of yard tracks and stopped beside a rectangular tower set beside the main line. He and Tony clattered up the steep wooden steps to the dimly lighted tower room.

Two men in grimy coveralls lounged on a bench at one side. John O'Conner, dispatcher, twisted away from his control board and grinned.

"Howdy, Marc. You fly over?"

"Practically. Hello, Baxter—Hobson."

Baxter waved to Marc. "Evenin', Mr. Jordan. John says you wanna see us."

"Yes. Glad to catch you. Tell me about the wreck."

"Ain't much to tell, sir. We're comin' into town right on time. I started to pinch her down fer the station like always on that curve. When I looked out, there was the car, right in front. We hit 'bout the time I seen it."

"Could you see anyone in the car?"

"Nope. No time to look. I big holed the air, but natu-rally, it didn't do no good. A truck derailed me onct. A car on the tracks scares hell outa me."

"You told O'Conner the car was standing there. Is that right?"

"Yeah. It wasn't movin'. I seen that much."

Marc turned to the fireman. "How about you, Hobson? Did you see the car?"

Hobson shook his head. "No. I can't see around the boiler on that curve. The crash was the first I knew about it."

Marc hunted through his pockets for a match to light his pipe. "A car standing there seems funny."

"There was another car, Mr. Jordan," continued the fireman.

The lighted match paused in mid-air.

"What?"

"There was another car. On my side. I seen the lights when we hit."

"This second car, was it standing too? Or coming up to the crossing?"

"Standin'. It was pretty close to the tracks."

"Then someone saw the wreck, Marc," said Tony.

"That's what I'm thinking. Wonder who it was."

"Probably scared stiff, and beat it."

"Could be. Maybe whoever it was will speak up, after they get over the shakes. Did either of you see anyone at the crossing when you stopped?"

Baxter shook his head. "We run by quite a piece. Can't stop on a dime, you know. We stayed with the engine and never did see the wreck."

"Holland didn't mention a second car, so it must've left before he got there." Marc sucked on his pipe thought-fully. "Thanks, fellows. Glad you stopped at the tower. Coming, Tony?"

Marc stepped through the door and clattered down the steps. Tony shrugged, grimaced at O'Conner, and followed.

"Away we go. Where to now, sir?" he asked meekly.

"Elm Way," replied Marc, starting the car with a jerk.

The crossing was dark and deserted when they returned. The night sounds of frogs and insects made the only break in the silence. Marc stopped the car directly on the tracks. He held the clutch in neutral and released the brake. Immediately the car gathered speed and coasted away from the track. He tried it again and again, stopping at different spots, but always with part of the car over the railroad. Each time the car coasted clear.

"What the devil are you up to?" demanded Tony. "Waiting for another train so we'll be killed too?"

"Doesn't something strike you funny?"

"Yes! You! Fooling around a railroad crossing. Ha-ha!"

"For a doctor, a psychiatrist, you're dumb, Tony my boy. A car won't stand on this crossing. The tracks're banked for the curve. The slope of the road coincides with the bank. There's enough grade so that a car won't stand unless the brakes are set! Dolly's car was parked here!"

"Judas!" exclaimed Tony. "Then you mean—?"

"Don't know what I mean," grunted Marc. He backed away from the crossing and stopped his car. Flashlight in hand, he strode rapidly along the track to the wreck. Dolly's car stood grotesquely upright. The right door had been removed with hack saws to get her body out. Marc peered into the front seat. He crawled in, distastefully trying to avoid the ugly brown splotches on the upholstery, and focused his light on the hand brake. After a brief examination he straightened.

"Hard to tell, the car's such a mess," he said, "but I think the hand brake's been set."

They walked back to the road. Marc stopped at the shallow ditch where he had noticed the tire tracks and footprints. The evidence was gone, in a maze of tracks made by other feet and wheels.

"Somehow, I'm glad I photographed that," he muttered. "Hope the picture turns out."

"If you're satisfied, let's go home. I'm tired."

"I'm not satisfied. Not by a long shot. We've chased our snake this far; let's kill it. I want to talk to Jane."

"Janey? Do you know what time it is? After two A.M. Her mama won't like!"

"Her mama'll have to like!" replied Marc grimly.

He turned the car, headed back toward Tenth Avenue and turned left. The Porter house was a blaze of light when they passed.

Marc glanced at the house without speaking. He drove half a dozen blocks farther and stopped before a modest home, not as elaborate as Porter's, but nonetheless substantial. It was dark and asleep.

He and Tony mounted the steps to the porch. Marc pressed the bell, and after a pause, pressed it again. In a few minutes a hall light flashed on, followed by the porch light. The door opened and a tousled head poked through the crack.

"Whadda ya want?" demanded an angry voice.

"Hello, Mr. Thompson. I'm Marc Jordan. May I see you a moment?"

"Oh, Jordan." The door swung open to disclose Thompson, a rumpled bathrobe clutched around his ample midriff. "Helluva time to go visitin'."

"I know it. I'm sorry to bother you. But I'd like very much to talk to Jane, if I may."

"Jane? At two A.M.? Are you crazy?"

"Maybe. I would like to see her—in your presence, of course."

"Well—I don't know if she'll come down."

"Please ask her. It's important."

"Oh, all right. Come on in."

"Thanks. You know Doctor Bodine?"

"Yeah. Hello, Doc."

Thompson snapped on a light in the living room and waved them in. Angrily he stamped up the stairs.

Marc smiled wryly. "A warm welcome!"

"What'd you expect?"

"A warm welcome."

After a short wait, Thompson returned.

"Siddown," he said. "She'll be here in a minute. What're you guys doin', prowlin' around this time of night? Innocent folks're in bed."

"That, Mr. Thompson, is where I want to be," said Tony fervently.

"Don't blame you for being annoyed." Marc stood in the center of the room and twirled a lock of hair around his finger. "I think you'll understand, though."

"Marc—Tony. You wolves!" Jane stood in the doorway clutching a frilly negligee around her waist, her fluffy hair pulled tight in a hair net. "It isn't fair to ogle a lady in this state!"

"Hi, Jane," said Marc. He pushed a chair out for her. "My humble apologies for getting you up. You look charming. I mean it."

"Cut the chatter," said Thompson roughly. "Come to the point."

"Yes, what is it, Marc? Is something the matter?"

"'Fraid so, Janey. Tell me what happened after you left the Ship's Hold tonight."

Jane stared at him, surprise dissipating the veil of sleep in her eyes.

"Why, nothing. Ted brought me straight home."

"Anything peculiar in his actions?"

Jane shrugged. "Peculiar? I don't know. You know Ted as well as I do. He's so quiet. Sort of—"

Tony nodded. "Nervous. High-strung. Intense. Sensitive. An introvert."

"I like Ted, a lot," she continued. "He's had a shock. He loved Dolly, you know. Her marrying Karl was a blow to him."

"We all know that. But what about tonight in particular?"

"He was depressed. He wanted to leave the party all of a sudden after Dolly and Karl left. He brought me home without an apology and hardly a good night. That isn't like him."

Marc paced the length of the room and back. "I can't get immune to breaking bad news," he muttered. He stopped in front of Jane. "Janey, after Ted left you tonight, he met Dolly. They went for a ride in her new car. The car was struck at Elm Way crossing by the Overland Flier. They were both killed!"

"Oh no!" gasped Jane. She shrank limply into the chair. "How horrible!"

Marc resumed his pacing. "Ordinarily, I wouldn't have bothered you tonight. But I don't understand what happened." He stopped again before her. "Now that you know that news, how did Ted behave?"

Jane shook her head, her eyes blank with shock.

"I can't believe it!" she whispered. "I just can't believe it."

"Did he give you any inkling that he expected to see Dolly?"

"No. None."

"Did you notice what he did when he left?"

She raised her eyes slowly to his. "Only that he turned his car around and drove back toward Porter's instead of on to his house. I didn't think anything of it, though. I thought maybe he was going back to town to get really drunk."

"I thought that's what must have happened, Jane."

"Poor, sweet, headstrong Dolly! Ted got her after all!"

"Yes," said Marc dryly, "he certainly did."

Thompson had been taking in the scene in silence. Suddenly he came to life.

"What's it mean, Jordan?"

Marc turned to him. "Two people dead. I represent the railroad, and there'll be an investigation."

"But don't you think we've investigated enough for to-night?" asked Tony. "I'm still tired."

"Almost," replied Marc. "We've bothered the Thompsons enough."

"I'm terribly sorry," said Jane. "Wonder if I should go to the Porters'?"

"Don't think so. There'll be time tomorrow. Thanks, Jane, and Mr. Thompson. Goodnight."

Marc sat for a moment before he started the car.

"Tony," he said, "you and Miriam left the party after Ted and Jane. Right?"

"Right."

"You went straight to the Porters'. Right?"

"Right."

"Karl said he did, and Jane says Ted brought her direct-ly home. Assuming that you each took about the same time to get here, you must've all arrived in the neighborhood in just about the same order that you left the Ship's Hold. Right?"

"Right."

"Do you know whether Ted's car was parked beside the Porter house when you left Miriam?"

"I don't know, Marc. I've been trying to think. I was in a bit of a daze. I've heart strings tied into the Porter manse, too, you know."

Marc laid his hand on Tony's knee.

"Tony," he said, "I hope that you aren't hurt, deeply, before this is over."

"What do you mean?"

"Nothing! Let's go see Miriam. Maybe she'll remember the car."

"Please, Marc. Let's not bother her any more tonight."

"I won't sleep unless I find out."

"You won't sleep anyway, you lawyer!"

Marc spun the car around and roared back the six blocks to the Porters'.

"Judas!" said Tony as they climbed out. "For years I'll be having nightmares about the squeak in your door hinge."

As they mounted the veranda they could see Miriam reclining on the davenport with her head on her arms. Marc opened the door and spoke softly.

"Miriam!"

Startled, she raised her head. Her face was haggard, tear-stained and weary.

He stepped quietly into the room and stopped beside her.

"Oh, Marc," she whispered.

"When Tony brought you home tonight, did you notice Ted's car parked on the side street?"

She pressed her hand to her forehead and thought for a moment. "No, Marc, I didn't see it."

"You're sure?"

She nodded. "Maybe it was there, but I didn't see it."

Tony stood in the door staring mutely at Miriam. Marc joined him.

"Goodnight, Miriam," he said. "Keep your chin up."

Once more they climbed into the car and headed home.

"What're you stewing about, Marc?"

He glared at the road.

"Tony," he said, "I think the wreck tonight was no accident."

"No accident?"

"The car was stopped on the crossing deliberately."

"By whom?"

"Ted!"

"Oh no, Marc! I can't believe it."

"What other explanation is there?" demanded Marc fiercely. "He's the type who could do it, isn't he?"

"Yes, but—"

"How else could it be? A car won't stand on the crossing. We proved that."

"You need a rest. A long one. You're seeing black spots."

Grimly, for the third time that night, Marc eased his car into the garage.

"Maybe. Anyway, no use talking about it. It'll just stir up trouble. It looked like a very convincing accident."

Tony slowly started up the steps. Marc fished his photographic kit out of the back seat.

"See you later," he said.

"Aren't you going to bed?"

"Not yet. Want to develop this film."

"Judas!" said Tony.

4

A plume of steam curled above a fussy switch engine sorting freight. A line of box cars stood on a storage track waiting its turn to go. A finger of smoke lay along the roof of a speeding passenger train that pounded across a bridge and disappeared behind a low hill.

Marc sat at a window in the top floor of the office building, his feet on his desk, and stared at the panorama of railroad activity. His head was shrouded in a haze of pipe smoke.

The telephone at his elbow buzzed insistently.

"Jordan speaking."

"Anderson. Police headquarters."

"Good morning, Jerry. How's the inspector? Crime wave under control?"

"Yeah. Say, Jordan, about this guy you fellows bumped off—"

"We bumped off?"

"Well, your choochoo chopped him up, but good!"

"Oh. What about him?"

"He don't seem to have no relations in town. I don't know what to do with his personal effects. There's a watch and some money in his billfold. Do you know how to find his family?"

49

"I don't think he had any, Jerry. His father and mother are dead. He was a lone wolf. Porter might know. Want me to find out for you?"

"Yeah. Be a help if you would."

"Be glad to. His car should be taken care of, too."

"That's right. Where is it?"

"Parked on the side street near Porter's."

"Why don't you drive it to a garage? Or bring it down here? We'll keep an eye on it till you dig up somebody to turn it over to."

"I don't have the keys. If you'll send someone over with them, I'll take care of it."

"What keys?"

"Aren't the car keys in his pocket?"

"Nope. No keys."

"Are you sure?"

"Heck yes. We emptied his pockets. There ain't no keys here."

"That's funny. I'll hunt up a mechanic and get it off the street."

"Much obliged, Jordan."

Marc watched the freight engine for ten minutes. He pulled an enlarged photograph from a drawer and examined it. Reaching a sudden decision, he picked up the phone.

"Police headquarters."

"Let me speak to Anderson, please."

There was a short pause.

"Yeah?"

"Jerry, Jordan again."

"Now what?"

"I've a request to make. I'd like to borrow Ted Arthur's shoes."

"What?"

"You heard me."

"I did. That takes the prize for screwy questions. What the devil you want 'em for?"

"I've a hunch. May I borrow them?"

"I guess so. Don't see no harm in it."

"I'll be right over."

Marc stuffed the picture in his pocket, donned his hat and coat and hurriedly left the office. He studied the picture again while waiting for the elevator. His car was parked in the lot beside the office, and he drove to the Municipal Building.

He waved to the desk man, an old friend, mounted the stairs three at a time to the second floor and burst unceremoniously into Anderson's office.

Anderson, a short, round man with a shiny head and thick-lensed glasses, sat hunched at a chipped desk. A pair of black oxfords, mud- and blood-smeared, reposed on a newspaper on the desk. The thick glasses gave Anderson's eyes a permanently startled expression; they were even more startled than usual when he turned from the shoes to Marc.

He grunted. "Howdy, Jordan. You gettin' psychic again?"

Marc picked up the shoes distastefully. "Maybe. These Arthur's shoes?"

"Yeah. I'm sure curious to know what you want 'em fer."

"I want to try an experiment. As you say, I'm psychic— or psychopathic!"

"You won't talk, huh?"

Marc shook his head. "Not yet, Jerry. Maybe I'm wrong. I hope I am wrong. If so, there's no reason to start rumors. If not, I'll be seeing you!"

"Okay, you close-mouthed son-of-a-gun! Get out of here. I got work to do."

Marc grinned at him. "Your hospitality simply overwhelms me. Thanks for the shoes. I'll return them later."

"Drop 'em in the river if you want to."

Marc wrapped the shoes in the newspaper and tucked the bundle under his arm.

"I won't do that, Jerry. They could be important. 'Bye."

He hurried to his car and again joined the stream of morning traffic. As rapidly as he dared, he drove toward the residential district. He turned into Elm Way, and stopped behind a tow car parked at the crossing.

A half-dozen men stood around the wreck of Dolly's car, earnestly debating what to do next. So far, obviously, nothing had been done.

"Hello, Mac," said Marc, joining the group.

A short, sandy-haired, powerfully built man looked up. He was proprietor of "Mac's Garage—Storage and Service." They'd had dealings in the past.

"How do, Mr. Jordan. Just tryin' to figger how we can get this wreck outa here."

"It's quite a long way to the road. Can you get your tow car in?"

"Mebbe. Ditch's pretty soft, though. Been thinkin' we could mebbe make a corduroy road over it with them ties."

"That's your problem, Mac. I won't hold you up. I just want to look this thing over by daylight."

Marc walked slowly around the car, studying it from all angles. He went carefully over the door on the driver's side. It was scratched and dirt-smeared like the rest of the car, but there were several brown splotches that weren't mud. He picked at them gingerly.

A piece of black cloth was hooked to the torn metal near the running board. He pulled it loose and tucked it into his pocket. He tried to turn the door handle, but it was bent and wedged fast. Then he reached through the broken window and tried to move the emergency brake. It too was stuck.

He stepped back, tamped his pipe full of tobacco, and touched a match to it. The workmen stood silent during his examination.

"A mess, eh, Mr. Jordan?" said Mac.

"A nasty accident," replied Marc. "Two of my good friends were killed. The girl was to be married today."

"Yeah. I seen it in the papers. Tough."

"It's all yours, Mac. I'm through."

"Right. We'll see if we can get her out."

Marc walked back to his car, trailing a stream of smoke, got out the bundle containing Ted's shoes and his box of camera equipment, and walked along the side of the road until he found a spot where the earth in the ditch was firm, moist and smooth. He unpacked the camera, fussed with the adjustments, and sighted through the range finder at the ditch.

Satisfied, he went to the car and squatted on the running board. Removing his shoes, he struggled to worm his long feet into Ted's shoes. Aversion twisted the corners of his mouth. After considerable tugging and stamping, he was able to walk, unsteadily and painfully, back to the ditch and through the spot he had selected.

He put his own shoes on again, speedily and with a sigh of relief. Then he aimed the camera at the fresh footprints and took several pictures.

By the time he had finished this strange maneuvering, the tow car was growling and grunting, and the wreck was moving toward the road on an improvised skid made of ties. Marc watched the operation for a moment.

Starting for the crossing, he examined the track and road bed foot by foot. Muttering inaudibly, he joined Mac beside the truck.

"Looks like you made it, Mac."

"That's right, Mr. Jordan. Have her out in a minute."

"Could you or one of your men go to Porter's with me?"

"Guess so. What fer?"

"Arthur left his car there. We can't find his keys and want to move the car. If you can fix it somehow so it'll run, we'll take it to the police garage."

"Sure, I'll go. These guys can handle this job now." Mac gave his men instructions, then climbed into the seat beside Marc.

"That car's junk," he said. "A shame. How'd it happen?"

Marc shrugged. "How does any crossing accident happen? They got in front of a train."

"Damn fools. Think they got the right of way."

"It hits me pretty hard. They were friends. We were all on a party last night."

Mac clucked his tongue. "Too bad. . . . This the one?" he asked as Marc pulled up in front of Ted's car.

Marc nodded. While Mac set about the business of tinkering with the ignition, Marc squatted beside the left front wheel and examined the tire. He had hardly begun when the motor turned over and broke into a steady purr.

"Gosh, Mac. That didn't take long," he said.

"Tell you, Mr. Jordan, it ain't hard to start a car. You push the clutch with your left foot, turn the ignition key, step on the starter. Works almost every time."

"Huh?" Marc peered through the open window and stared blankly at the dash. "Where were those keys?" he demanded.

"In the ignition."

"Let me get this straight," said Marc slowly. "You got into the car, and found the key in the lock?"

"That's right."

"Well, I'll be darned!"

"What's funny about that?"

"They weren't there last night. I looked."

"So someone put 'em back."

"Yes, Mac, someone did. Let me see them."

He passed over the key folder. It was a leather affair, with the initials "T.E.A." embossed on the flap. A pocket in the back held Ted Arthur's driving license. Marc handed it back.

"Will you take the car to the city garage? Tell Anderson I sent you."

"Sure."

"Just a minute. I want to look at this tire."

He scrutinized the tire carefully, picked at a loose flap of rubber and ran his finger along a narrow cut. Straightening up, he opened the door and studied the floor mat under Mac's feet. He pried several small gray pebbles out of the corrugated running board cover, rolled them in the palm of his hand and dropped them into his pocket.

"Okay, Mac, take it away. Thanks."

Marc watched the car disappear around the corner, his face wearing a puzzled frown, then walked slowly along the path toward the Porter house. A huge white crepe hung beside the door. Blinds were drawn at every window. Even the garage doors were all closed. The whole place had an air of silent sorrow.

At the step he paused, turned back to the street, and slid behind the wheel of his car. His face wooden, he drove home.

In the basement of his apartment, he entered a cubbyhole in the corner, set his camera box on a table, and adjusted a heavy black curtain across the door. Working rapidly, he mixed a pan of chemicals and in the pale red glow of a dark light developed the film from his camera.

When the negatives were in the hypo bath, he turned on the light. The pictures were all good. With a grunt of satisfaction, he finished the hypo wash, followed by a rinse in a running water tank. Gently, he squeezed the excess water from the clearest film between sheets of blotting paper, pinned the negative to a board with thumb tacks and set a small fan so that its blast struck the film.

Every few minutes Marc touched the film with the impatience of a cook waiting for the kettle to boil. In fifteen minutes it was dry. He quickly made a print.

His fingers trembled when he laid the print on the table top, squeezed the water from it, and turned on the light. He pulled the picture of the previous evening from his pocket and laid it beside the new one. Avidly, he glared first at one and then the other.

Suddenly, he picked up the two pictures and stuffed them into his pocket, climbed into his car, and drove to the Municipal Building.

Anderson was busy reading a report when Marc burst into the office. He glanced up in annoyance.

"Your manners are as bad's ever, Jordan."

Without replying, Marc spread the pictures out on Anderson's desk, shoved his hat to the back of his head and fumbled for his pipe.

"Cast your experienced eyes on these, Jerry. Tell me what you see."

Anderson studied the prints. "Good pictures, Jordan. What'm I supposed to see?"

"Footprints!"

"Well, well! So they are. Amazing!"

"Tell me whether or not these prints are like these." Marc pointed first to one picture and then the other.

Anderson examined the pictures more slowly.

"Yes," he replied, "I'd say so. What of it?"

"Um-mm." Marc sank into a chair beside the desk and propped his feet on a corner. "I thought so too."

He sucked his pipe for several minutes. "I want to tell you a story, Jerry."

"Better be good. I'm busy."

"Listen. Then you can tell me. Dolly Porter and Ted Arthur were killed in an auto wreck last night."

"That, my boy, is news!"

"In the first place," continued Marc, "it's all-fired strange that they were together at all. Dolly was to be married today to Karl Snyder."

"A farewell party. You just ain't been around!"

"That's what I thought, at first. The wreck looks like an accident, the kind that happens every day. But Baxter, the hogger, saw the car just before he hit it. He says it was standing still. Now a car won't stand there by itself. Doc Bodine and I went back last night and tried it. There's enough grade so that a car will coast at a good clip, unless the brakes're set."

"So what?"

"Don't you see? The car wasn't moving, so it wasn't a case of stupidly driving in front of the train. If the engine had died, all the driver would've had to do would be kick out the clutch and coast in the clear. Therefore the only logical conclusion is that the car was parked deliberately!"

"You figgerin' that one of 'em wanted to die?"

"That's the conclusion I reached last night. I thought Ted drove to the Porters', picked up Dolly with some kind of a song and dance, and deliberately stopped in front of the train. Everyone in the neighborhood knows that train. It always blows for the crossing. They set their clocks by it."

"Story's interesting, anyhow."

"If I were sure of that, Jerry, I wouldn't be here. There'd be no sense in stirring up more heartaches. But I'm not. You didn't find Ted's keys in his pocket!"

"Ye gods! Here we go. What's that got to do with it?"

"Ted always locks his car. It's a standing joke. And yet his car, parked at the Porters', was not locked. And the keys weren't there either, last night."

"Jordan, you're building up something. Spit it out. I'm busy."

"Between the time when I looked at the car last night and this morning, some one put the keys back!"

"You just didn't see 'em last night."

"Because they weren't there!" snapped Marc. "There's more to it. Hobson, the fireman, saw a second car behind Dolly's. When the conductor got back to the wreck, the second car was gone.

"I photographed the wreck. Always do, if possible. On some kind of a hunch, I also photographed the marks of that second car in the ditch, and the footprints to and from it. It's one of those pictures. This morning they're gone. Washed out by the milling mob.

"I borrowed Ted's shoes, remember? Today I went back there and made new prints, using his shoes, and photographed them. They're on the other pictures. They're the same as some of the prints on the first picture."

"Some of 'em?"

"Look at the first picture again. There are two kinds of prints. Ted's shoes left the second car, but someone else came back. Someone with big feet that wobbled like he was drunk."

Anderson examined the pictures again. "Maybe you're right."

"Of course I'm right!" Marc leaped to his feet and prowled around the office like a caged tiger. "Furthermore, the outside—the outside, mind you—of Dolly's car is smeared with blood. A piece of cloth was hooked in the running board.

"Here's what happened. Some of it's guesswork, but I'm positive of the general outline. Ted left the girl friend and drove by the Porters'. He spotted Dolly's car somewhere along the way, and on a heartsick impulse, followed. When he got to the Elm Way crossing, there it was on the tracks with a train coming. He stopped, leaped out of his own car, ran to her and tried to get her out, but didn't make it.

"Some murderous third person was lurking in the shadows, the one who drove Dolly there in the first place. The guy who made those wobbly footprints. As soon as the train passed, he got into Ted's car, drove it to the Porters' and vanished. Ted was no suicide! He wasn't even a dope! He was a hero. He tried to save Dolly and died in the attempt. You've got a slick, fiendish murder on your hands, Mr. Anderson!"

Anderson shined his bald pate with a big polka dot handkerchief.

"Nuts!" he said.

Marc leaned his fists on the desk and glared at Anderson with repressed fury.

"What do you mean—nuts?"

"I mean nuts. What was the coroner's verdict?"

"Death by accident."

"That's good enough for me."

"But, Jerry—" Marc stamped to the door and back. He beat the desk with his palm. "The facts don't add up to an accident."

"What facts? You ain't got none. You're guessing."

"How about the tire marks, and the footprints?"

"Don't prove a thing. Sit down, Jordan. I'll explain it to you, slow. What if that is Arthur's car? How do you know when the track was made? Maybe he was lookin' the ground over the day before."

"But the footprints?"

"Maybe they're his, maybe not. Suppose they are. He walked to the track through the ditch, back on the hard-surfaced road. Someone else made the others, any time."

"How do you explain the missing keys, which later turned up in the car?"

Anderson rocked back in his chair and pulled at what should have been hair. Marc thrust his hands deep in his pockets and glared at him.

"So," he said, snapping the words out bitterly, "you'll do nothing."

"Nothing. Jordan, be sensible. You ain't got no proof."

"I think it's proof."

"Oh, rats! Porter's a big man in Calumet. I got my reputation to think of. I can't stir up a scandal on what you think you got."

Marc stared at him for a moment, turned and left without replying.

5

The orchestra on the poop deck of the Ship's Hold struggled in a most un-nautical manner. The tiny dance floor was packed with courageous dancers.

Doctor Anthony Bodine, Calumet's leading psychiatrist, solicitously held the arm of Miss Porter, and helped her across the swaying gangplank to the pilot house. His eyes swept the crowded tables, the rhythm-drunk humanity on the floor, and turned ruefully to Miriam.

An obsequious headwaiter tripped up the steps from the deck, his face deferential and apologetic.

"Good evening, Doctor Bodine," he said. "Sorry, but I don't believe I have a table. We're busy tonight. If you'll wait in the forward cabin, I'm sure I'll have one for you soon."

"You're packin' me in, Charles," replied Tony. "We'll wait. . . . Hey! Let's join them!" He pointed to the couple at a small table in a corner. Marc and Nora, their heads close together, sat in earnest conversation.

"Friends of yours?" asked Charles.

Tony nodded. "I think they'll admit knowing us."

Charles beamed. "Splendid. Come this way, please." Following him, they stopped beside the table.

"Boo!" said Tony.

Marc looked up and sprang to his feet. "Oh! Hello, folks."

"May we join you? Charle's fresh out of tables."

"Of course," replied Nora. She gave Miriam an affectionate pat. "Glad to see you."

Charles produced a pair of chairs and the four crowded around the tiny table.

"Double Scotch, Charles, and an old-fashioned. That right, Miriam?"

She nodded.

"Well," continued Tony, "surprised to see you two cherubs in this den of iniquity. Getting fancy ideas, eh?"

Marc smiled. "My little Irish girl friend! For years I've kept her out of here."

"Marc Jordan!" exclaimed Nora. "That's a vile, slanderous insinuation. You suggested it yourself."

"It's a shame for us to butt in on your party," said Miriam.

Nora turned to her. "Oh, no, Miriam. Not at all."

"We're going soon," said Marc, lighting his pipe and glancing at her. "Mr. Porter's private secretary must get her beauty sleep."

"Marcus," said Tony, fanning the cloud of smoke that fogged his eyes, "what're you going to do when St. Peter makes you park that garbage incinerator outside the pearly gates?"

Marc chuckled. "You and I won't need to worry about St. Peter. Fact, that holds for most of us." He gave Miriam a slow, searching look.

"Speak for yourself, Marc," retorted Nora.

"Murder will out," said Tony, raising his glass.

"Will it?" murmured Marc.

Nora hurriedly gathered up her gloves and handbag. "We must go, Marc. It's late."

"Right. We'll will you the place."

"I hope we aren't chasing you away," said Miriam.

"Not at all. You'll take care of the check, Tony, I presume?"

"You presume wrong, you four-flusher!"

Marc clapped him on the shoulder. "Thanks," he said.

Tony watched them disappear through the hatch.

"What a guy," he said. "A cat- and railroad-loving lawyer! Only one like him."

"Wonder when they'll get married?"

Tony chuckled. He waved imperiously to the waiter, and pointed to his empty glass.

"Nora's stubborn. Her father's railroaded all his life and mostly worked nights. Says she'll have none of it."

"She'll come around."

"Haven't seen Karl lately. Still away?"

Miriam nodded. "Dad told him to get out of town for a few weeks. He'll be back Monday. He was upset."

Tony held a match for her cigarette, and his own.

"Have you missed him?" His impersonal smile hid a very personal interest.

Miriam returned his glance soberly. She patted his hand with her fingertips. "Patient doing nicely, Doctor!"

"Doctor prescribes more of the same specific. Dance?" His heart gave a flutter.

She looked at the solid welter of humanity, and made a face.

"No, thanks! The orchestra sounds better from here."

"You should bring along your harmonica. Play a solo and earn our drinks."

Miriam giggled. "I'm taking lessons!"

"Huh?"

"Really. Seven to eight on Thursdays. It's fun."

Tony rose and bowed formally. "Madam, it is indeed an honor to have known you when!"

Miriam laughed. "Oh, sit down, silly." She glanced at her watch. "We must go, Tony. It *is* late."

"Whatever you say."

Tony was silent during the drive home. He glanced repeatedly at Miriam. Her thoughts were miles away, and he wisely refrained from interfering.

At the corner of the veranda he stood with her a moment in the shadows of a lilac bush. He put his hands on her shoulders and gently tucked her coat collar under her chin. Their eyes met. The desire to press her to him was almost uncontrollable.

"Thanks, Tony. It was a lovely evening."

He hesitated a moment. "Good night, Miriam. See you soon."

He whistled softly under his breath as he drove away.

He dawdled through the business district, on an impulse decided he was hungry. He stopped at a lunch wagon and had a hamburger before continuing.

As he turned from the alley into the garage, the lights blinked on. Marc ran down the steps, tieless and with his tousled hair poking out from under his hat, and hurried toward his own car. He stopped in the glare of Tony's lights and waved for him to stop, then climbed quickly into the seat beside Tony.

"Back out!" he said imperiously.

Tony stared at him in amazement. "For Pete's sake, what's the matter with you?"

"Head for the Porters'. Quick!"

"The Porters'?"

"Don't argue!" Marc barked the words out. "Get going."

"But, Judas, what's wrong? Is someone hurt?"

Marc stared grimly at the road. "Not yet, I hope. Someone took a pot shot at Miriam. She just called."

Tony's complacence vanished. The accelerator hit the floor with a thud and the car careened crazily through the deserted streets. Skidding into the drive, Tony stopped with a screech of brakes.

The Porter house was ablaze with lights. Marc, with Tony close at his heels, ran onto the veranda and burst through the door.

Cynthia huddled on the davenport, her body jerked by uncontrolled sobs. Miriam cushioned her mother's head on her shoulder and tried to comfort her, gnawing her lips to check her own hysteria.

She looked at Marc wildly, her eyes round with shock. A shuddering spasm shook her slender body.

"Oh, Marc, I'm glad you came," she whispered.

Tony leaned over her and pressed her hungrily to himself for a moment. Then he pulled her gently away from her mother. He slapped Cynthia's cheeks, softly at first, then roughly.

"Stop it, Cynthia!" he ordered. "Stop it!"

She suddenly reared back against the cushions, her eyes glazed with terror as she stared at Tony. Then her clutching arms encircled Miriam and her sobs were renewed.

"My baby, my baby!"

"This must stop," said Tony briskly. "Get away from her, Miriam. Get her a drink. Take one yourself!"

Gently but firmly he forced Cynthia to stretch out, and tucked a blanket around her. When Miriam returned, he held her head and forced a few swallows through her twisted lips. Slowly Cynthia relaxed and her sobbing abated.

Tony shot a look of concern at Miriam.

"How are you?" he asked. He tried to mask his own alarm behind professional calm.

Miriam sank into a chair and pressed her palms to her face. "I'm all right. Take care of Mother."

Marc had been examining the shattered window. He turned now to Miriam.

"What happened, Miriam?" he asked quietly.

She shuddered. "I don't know, Marc, exactly. I was reading the paper. I got up and started to go into the hall. Just a few seconds afterwards, the window glass was shattered and a bullet thumped into the cushion. I was so frightened!"

"Were you alone?"

"Yes," she said.

"Where are the rest of this family?"

"Dad and Harrison are searching the grounds."

"You called the police?"

"Dad did. I screamed, I guess. Then I called you. It was all I could think of to do."

Outwardly Marc showed none of the turmoil of doubt and fear that seethed within him. Something about this frightened girl—

His thoughts were interrupted by the slamming door. Porter stamped in, his bathrobe flapping and a flashlight in his hand. His rumpled hair, the livid tangle of veins beside his nose, his grim eyes bespoke outraged fury. He laid the flashlight on a table by the door and glowered at Marc.

"Where're the police? I'm a taxpayer. Why don't I get protection? The lazy devils! I'll have somebody's hide."

"They'll be along," said Marc quietly.

"Not a sign of anything now. Naturally. Time them birds get here, the place'll be as empty as a robbed grave."

"Have you searched the grounds?"

"Every cussed inch. Not a thing, not even a footprint."

"You heard the shot?"

"Yeah. Then Miriam's scream to wake the dead."

Marc, still puzzled, turned back to Miriam. "How long had you been reading before the shot was fired?"

She looked at him uncertainly. "I don't know. Fifteen or twenty minutes."

"Did you have any warning? Hear any strange sounds?"

She shook her head.

Marc bent over the davenport and examined the small, ragged hole in the upholstery. Turning, he faced the shattered window in the opposite wall. He walked slowly into the hall and, hand on knob, started involuntarily at a shadowy figure on the veranda.

"Oh! Hello, Joel. You startled me."

"Hi, Marc. What goes?"

Peering, Marc tried to see the face hidden by a slouch hat. "Just get home?"

"Yeah. What's the excitement?"

"Where've you been?"

"None of your damn business. You going to tell me what you're doing?"

"Better find out for yourself, Joel."

A police siren wailed a warning to all evildoers. The car slewed into the drive with a great show of official diligence. Marc ignored the onrushing law and stepped to the lawn outside the broken window.

Despite his height, the sill obstructed his view of the room. The davenport was below the line of sight. Porter, pacing wrathfully to and fro, was visible, and he could just see Tony's hair.

Marc continued along the path to the street. Higher than the lawn and house, this point afforded an excellent view of the room. He stooped and sighted over the waist-high hedge. The hole in the davenport could be easily seen.

Following the hedge, Marc walked along the side street to the end of the Porter domain and turned into an alley. His hand had scarcely touched the rear gate when a low, menacing snarl brought him up short. A finger of light from his torch showed Rags, lips drawn back and chin flat on the ground, crouching beyond the fence.

"Easy, Rags," said Marc soothingly. "Right on duty, eh, boy?"

Rag's brush raised upright and swung back and forth. The snarl changed to a friendly "Woof!"

Squatting beside him, Marc fondled the big head and tickled his jaws. Rags shook himself and turned back to the business of devouring a chunk of meat.

Marc prowled around the grounds. He expected to find nothing, and he was right.

Voices inside the house were loud when he mounted the steps. Watching the turbulent scene, he couldn't repress an inward chuckle.

Tony left his post beside Cynthia as Marc entered, and advanced on Porter and Anderson. His face, usually bland and friendly, now radiated indignation.

"You guys, shut up! There are two frightened, hysterical women here, and you scrap like fighting cocks. Now cut it out!"

Porter jerked a disdainful thumb at Anderson. "With an ignorant nincompoop like this for a police inspector, why shouldn't I be mad? What's he done? What's he gonna do?"

Anderson gnawed the stump of a cigar in lieu of a blasphemous retort, restraining himself by a mighty effort.

"We'll do what we can, Mr. Porter. I'll put out a dragnet. We'll get that trigger-happy mug. And I'll leave a man on guard here tonight."

"You'll do more than that, my good man. You'll put a guard on my house until you find the crook, or I'll see the commissioner! Good notion to do it anyhow. Darned if I want some lunatic pot-shooting at my family!"

Anderson nodded hurriedly. "Okay, okay. I'll take care of it. Now don't you worry, Mr. Porter; we'll straighten this out. Just routine. Probably have our man by morning."

"You'd better!"

"Come on, Pete." Anderson indicated the door with a sidewise jerk of his head. "Let's go."

Amused and sympathetic, Marc watched Anderson's retreat. Porter's anger puzzled him a little. It burned so constantly, with such white heat. Of course, a bullet out of the night was no joking matter.

Porter arrested his prowling in front of Joel.

"Where you been?"

"Out!"

"Hangin' around the Purple Pot, I'll bet. Were you?"

Joel nodded diffidently. "I stopped in for a beer."

"What did you use for money? You were broke yesterday."

"Fellow paid back some dough he borrowed."

Porter shook a stiff finger at him. "Young man—"

A sound, half gurgle, half sigh, from Cynthia interrupted him. She struggled to a sitting position and pressed a palm against each eye.

"Please, Don," she murmured, "don't. Leave him alone."

"Okay," he growled, squatting on the davenport beside her and patting her shoulder.

Methodically, Marc tamped his pipe full of tobacco. Tony took the cue and shook out a cigarette for himself, offered one to Miriam. Her trembling fingers fumbled with the pack and a pathetic wisp of a smile thanked him.

"I would like to know what happened," muttered Marc, half to himself. He sank into a big chair and hooked a knee over the arm.

"Some ape took a shot at Miriam," said Porter. "That's what."

Tears welled up in Cynthia's eyes. She gestured to Tony. "A cigarette, and a drink. I need both!"

"That's the smartest request yet," replied Porter, lumbering into the kitchen.

"Miriam," said Marc, "did Rags sound off any time before the shot was fired?"

Miriam shook her head.

"He's a good dog. Few minutes ago, he snarled the second I laid my hand on the gate. So the intruder must have stayed on the street, or Rags would've had him."

Porter returned with a tray of glasses. Tony snatched one. "Brother, I need this too!"

"Don," continued Marc, "how long was it between the shot and Miriam's scream?"

Porter stared curiously at him, and shrugged. "Can't say. Few seconds, maybe."

"You went into the hall, Miriam?"

Again she nodded. "I guess I didn't yell right away. I was too frightened even to breathe for a minute."

Marc rose, strode to the davenport and ran his finger around the jagged bullet hole. His eyes roved over the room and lighted on a paper knife on the mantel. With it, he probed the recess and finally worked loose a lead pellet. Thoughtfully he rolled it in the palm of his hand, then dropped it into his vest pocket.

He twisted a curl in his forelock as he walked slowly back to his seat.

"It's a miracle," he said, "that you weren't killed. And miracles shouldn't happen."

6

Wrathful and impatient, Inspector Anderson thumbed rapidly through a pile of papers. He read the top letter again, squinting through his thick glasses. Satisfied, he snapped a rubber band around the file, pitched it into a mail basket and picked up a second similar file. He glanced up to see the tall, slightly stooped figure of Marc Jordan standing in the doorway.

Anderson waved. "Come on in, Jordan."

Marc ambled to a round-backed chair beside Anderson, sank into it, and propped his feet on the desk.

"Morning, Jerry. Hard at it?" Marc scrutinized a snag in one of his shoes.

Anderson grunted. "The wicked know no rest," he said sententiously.

Thoughtfully, Marc loaded his pipe. "Turn up anything up on the Porter shooting?" he asked.

"Yes and no. Mostly no. Picked up one shady character in the neighborhood. Guy named Meegan. Nothin' on him, though. Had to let him go."

"You've had a patrol on Porter's house all night?"

"Yeah. And tonight. And tomorrow night. What the devil does he think I am? A prophet? If I had a man at every likely trouble spot, half the people in Calumet'd be workin' for me, watchin' the other half."

"Porter's house looks like a trouble spot."

"Aw, some crackpot. Country's full of 'em."

"This chap Meegan?"

Anderson shrugged. "How should I know? He didn't have no gun, or nothing to hold him for."

"He could've ditched it somewhere."

"Sure he could. So could lots of other people."

"What's shady about him?"

"His looks. And he hangs out with a pack of hoodlums at the Purple Pot. Had him in on suspicion, couple months ago."

"Suspicion of what?"

"Guy on Beechwood thought he seen someone sneak through his garden."

"Beechwood. Anywhere near the Porters'?"

Anderson's eyes, magnified by his glasses, ogled Marc. He scratched his head. "Come to think of it, it was the other end of their block the call come from."

Imperturbably Marc blew a jet of smoke at the ceiling. "Remember what I said about the death of Dolly Porter and Ted Arthur last month?"

Perplexed, Anderson bounced the stump of a cigar from one corner of his mouth to the other.

"Still harpin' on that, huh? Suppose you figure some connection."

Marc's mouth formed a grim line. Suppressing his impatience with an effort, he stared at Anderson.

"Doesn't it strike you queer that a murderous attempt should be made on Miriam so soon after her sister's death?"

"Coincidence. Can't be anything else."

Marc shook his head. "I don't believe it. Something in or around the Porter menage stinks."

Anderson chuckled derisively. "Jordan, you're a nice guy. I like you. But you're nuts."

Disgustedly, Marc rose and wheeled around the office.

"Okay. Have it your way. What're you going to do about Meegan?"

"Nothin'. Nothin' I can do."

"Jerry—" commenced Marc. Then he changed his mind. Anderson worked according to his lights, if they were sometimes low wattage. He walked to the door and turned, hand on knob.

"That family're friends of mine. I'd like to help them. Keep me posted, will you?"

"Yeah. Beat it, and quit worryin'."

Marc stood indecisively on the sidewalk for a moment, then hurried to the corner and turned up Main Street. Long strides carried him rapidly through pedestrian traffic like a halfback running through a broken field.

Arriving at a tall office building, he took the elevator to the ninth floor. With the same long strides he covered the length of the corridor and stopped before a door labeled: "Thatcher Detective Agency."

Entering a small anteroom, he was met by the glare of an immaculately dressed, distinctively bald man with a cauliflower ear and extraordinarily long arms. Thatcher's receptionist, bodyguard and bouncer.

Despite long acquaintance, Marc flinched involuntarily.

"Howdy, Svenson," he said. "Thatcher in?"

"Yeah."

"May I see him?"

"Mebbe. I'll find out."

Svenson disappeared through an inner door; in a moment he returned and jerked a thumb toward the office.

"In here."

Marc sidled by the ape-like figure and regarded the man seated at the desk. A big man, with a solid mass of black hair crowding low over immensely piercing, narrow-slitted eyes. He sat, characteristically, with his hands palms down on the desk top. Otherwise the desk was innocent of any incumbrance. Idly, Marc wondered what secrets were hidden in that desk, and in the row of heavy steel cabinets that lined one wall. Interesting material, undoubtedly.

Thatcher returned his stare. "Come in, Jordan. What's on your mind?"

Marc squatted on a stiff-backed chair, tilted it against the wall and hooked his toes around the rungs.

"Good morning, Thatcher," he said, fishing for his pipe. "I need some help."

"Most people do," replied Thatcher in a flat tone. "Most of 'em come to me."

"Wisely," replied Marc dryly. He lit his pipe and polished the bowl with his thumb. "You've heard about the shooting fracas at the Porter home last night?"

"Yeah. What about it?"

"Friends of mine. Inspector Anderson's inclined to take the matter lightly as the prank of some dimwitted joker. What do you think about it?"

"I never have opinions, Jordan. Just facts. I find 'em out, and get paid for it."

A sardonic grin flitted across Marc's face and vanished. "I understand." He puffed thoughtfully for several minutes in silence. Thatcher, unmoving, watched him.

"I'm afraid, Thatcher, that hideous business is afoot. Frankly, I'm worried. The only progress Anderson's made is to pick up, and then turn loose, a gangster named Meegan who was haunting the neighborhood. Know him?"

Thatcher shrugged almost imperceptibly. "Heard of him."

"What've you heard?"

"If I had any information, I wouldn't give it out gratis."

Marc nodded. "By this time I should know you, Thatcher! Granted, Meegan's perhaps just a straw. But I'd like to know more about him. I'd like you to undertake the investigation of his private life."

"You know, Jordan, that I don't mess with criminal cases. Private evil, that's my meat."

"Yes. But in view of certain small favors I've done for you, perhaps you'd make an exception."

"My gratitude doesn't run to free detective service," said Thatcher dryly. "'Specially if the job's a stinker."

"Maybe it isn't a stinker. I've nothing on Meegan but a hunch. As for expenses, I've an angel in mind who'll foot the bill, I think."

"What do you want?"

"I want you to tail Meegan, day and night. He's probably had experience with both ends of a tail, so you'll have to use good men. I don't want him to know about it if it can be helped."

"That I can do. What else?"

"I want his history. Where's he from, and particularly why he's here in Calumet."

Thatcher removed his hands from the desk top and, touching fingertip to fingertip, formed a tent.

"And you'll pay, huh?"

"I'll personally guarantee expenses for twenty-four hours." A tingle of excitement ran through Marc. He rose suddenly and paced about the office. Finally he stopped opposite Thatcher. "If I can't make other arrangements, I'll let you know. How about it?"

Thatcher's eyes raised slowly. "All right, Jordan. I'll take the job on one condition."

"Yes?"

"That I don't get any bad publicity."

"I'll see to that." Marc resumed his pacing. "All I want is information. You can be trusted, Thatcher. That's why I'm here. Anderson thinks I'm nuts. Maybe. But unless there's more rumpus at the Porter homestead, I'm a Chinaman."

"You want me to keep an eye on Meegan?"

Marc scowled fiercely. "Not one eye—two! Watch him every second. Don't let your man put him to bed and go home, expecting to pick him up in the morning. Stay with him all night. Especially at night. It shouldn't take long to find out if he's suspicious. And keep me informed of his actions and habits. If he makes any kind of a move toward the Porters', let me know—quick!"

"Okay. I'll take care of it."

"Thanks. I appreciate your help."

Marc nodded to Thatcher, dodged by Svenson, and returned to the street, where he retraced his steps.

Arriving at the railroad office building, he went directly to his car parked in a lot at the rear, drove through back streets to avoid the midday traffic and headed toward the lower part of the city.

Parking in the circular drive at the entrance to the Porter Manufacturing Company, he stared a moment unseeingly at the steering wheel. He knew what he wanted of Porter. Could he get it? Only one way to find out. He slid from behind the wheel, mounted the flight of steps and entered the lobby.

Pausing at the receptionist's desk, he nodded.

"Good morning, Miss Johnson. I'd like to see Mr. Porter, if I may."

She smiled at him. "He's in, Mr. Jordan, and I think he's free."

"If not, I'll annoy Nora a while. Thanks."

When he stepped into the room which opened off a short hall Nora glanced up, pleasure and surprise mingling in her eyes.

"Why, Marc! Good morning. What're you doing here?"

"I want to see your boss—and you."

"I get it. You want to see the boss."

"Is he in?"

"Yes. He'll see an important person like you, I'm sure."

She opened an inner door and spoke to Porter, then turned and smiled at Marc.

"Mr. Porter said to come right in."

"Sit down, Marc. Be with you in a second. Cigar?" Porter flipped open a humidor with one hand and reached for a telephone with the other. Marc shook his head, loaded his pipe instead while Porter issued a string of crisp instructions to some unseen assistant. When he had finished the conversation, he dropped the phone in place and turned expectantly to Marc.

"Now, what can I do for you?"

"Really, it's none of my business, Don. Kick me out if you like. But I'm concerned about the shooting affair last night."

"Hell's bells, so'm I! Bullets flying around are nothing to laugh off."

"I've just been talking to Anderson. He doesn't have much to offer."

"That incompetent pup! Why we tax payers put up with such nitwits is beyond me. That's the trouble with this country. Too many official nincompoops."

Marc laughed. "You elect them, Don. You and I. You're too hard on Anderson. He's a hard-working, conscientious, honest cop. His only fault is his lack of imagination."

"Rats. I don't believe it."

"D'you have any idea who took a pot shot at Miriam last night?"

Porter ran his fingers through his hair and shook his head.

"If I did, I'd have him under lock and key."

"Cynthia and Miriam all right this morning?" He watched Porter closely.

"Guess so. I left before they were up, but when I called a while ago, Miriam said things were quiet."

Marc slouched in the soft chair and extended his feet full length.

"I don't like it, Don."

"You don't like it! How do you think I feel?"

"Anderson turned up one lead—maybe. A mighty thin one, but a lead."

"Yeah? What?"

"He picked up a doubtful character—you might say hoodlum—named Meegan near your place. Had to let him go, though, for lack of evidence."

Porter stabbed the air with his finger. "See? What'd I tell you? He let him go! Of all the idiotic—"

"He had to, Don. He can't arrest a man and hold him without some grounds. He's right. I'd consider him a lead only because there were no others."

Porter eyed him shrewdly. "What're you hiding in that nimble brain of yours, Marc? You're a cool hand. You wouldn't be here wastin' your time and mine for nothing."

Marc blew a string of smoke rings. He rose slowly and stood at the window staring at the street.

"You're shrewd yourself, Don. Also right." He returned to his seat. "I've been worried ever since—for some time. I expected something to happen. Not this, exactly. Not a shot out of the dark. But something."

Porter watched him, his eyes veiled and puzzled.

"You did? Why?"

"Psychic seizure, maybe. Can you think of any reason why Miriam should have been attacked?"

Porter's face wore a bewildered expression. "That's it. I can't. What reason could there be?"

"I'm asking you," said Marc dryly.

"Well," Porter took a cigar from the humidor and clipped the end, "I've made some enemies. Any successful businessman does." He waved at the beautifully appointed office. "You can see I'm successful. Why should some sorehead try to get to me by bopping Miriam? She's not my daughter. You knew that, didn't you?"

Marc hesitated. "Yes. I did know. D'you have any particular business associate in mind?"

"Are you pumping me, Marc?"

"Sorry, Don." He laughed softly. "It's not entirely idle curiosity. Fact is, I think something should be done about Meegan."

"What, for instance?"

"I think he should be watched."

"Isn't that Anderson's job?"

"Perhaps. Would be if he had reasons for suspicion. But he doesn't."

"I wouldn't be where I am if I didn't sometimes take advice. You got an idea? What is it?"

"I'd suggest that you engage a private detective to watch Meegan."

"You really think trailing this Meegan might help?"

"I don't know, Don. I've a hunch it will."

"But I don't trust private dicks."

"I talked to Thatcher a while ago. Know him personally. You can trust him. He's honest, at least with the person paying him. He'll take the job."

"I don't like to deal with those guys."

"I'll deal with him," said Marc softly. "Be glad to."

"What'll it cost?"

"Not too much. It'll be cheaper than a funeral. How much better for Dolly—" Marc almost bit his tongue in two.

A spasm of pain flicked across Porter's face. "Dolly? What about Dolly?"

"Nothing. I was thinking of something else."

"Well, all right, Marc. Tell Thatcher to go to work. You take care of it, will you? Report progress and send me the bill."

"You're wise, Don. I'll get along now. Things to do."

"Drop in again, Marc." Porter waved him out the door.

Pensively, Marc drove to the nearest drug store. He made his way to a phone booth in the corner.

The phone grated. "Hello!"

"May I speak to Thatcher, please?"

"Hold it."

In a moment Thatcher's voice came evenly over the wire.

"Thatcher speaking."

"Jordan. Green light on the job I spoke about, Thatcher. Expenses paid, and I'm to handle it. Remember the name of the target house?"

"Yes, I get you."

"Include the gentleman's son, same arrangement. One hundred per cent. Understand?"

"Uh! Mighty risky, Jordan. You're playing with fire."

"I know. I'm the fireman!"

"Okay. I'll take care of it."

7

Wearily, Marc dropped the magazine he'd been trying to read on the seat beside him and stretched. The train clattered through the night, a speeding oasis of light. He twisted in a futile attempt to find a comfortable position. The hard plush seats weren't built to suit his spare anatomy.

He rose and, clutching the seat backs for support, walked the length of the swaying car to the next, at the far end of which the train crew slouched, putting in time between chores. He dropped into a vacant seat, nodding to the men, pushed his hat to the back of his head and stretched his feet into the aisle.

"About on time tonight, Holland," he said, glancing at his watch.

"Yup. Be in Calumet right on the money."

"Ain't seen you around much, Mr. Jordan," said Adams, the brakeman. "Where you been?"

"Busy in town. You fellows've managed to keep out of trouble."

"I don't want no more like that auto wreck last month. Wow! Was that guy a mess! Made me sick to my stomach."

"Whatever come o' that, Mr. Jordan?" asked Holland.

Marc shrugged. "It's still unsettled. I don't know what's next."

The conversation veered to railroading, the fascinating train talk of railroaders everywhere. Marc loved it. He never tired of chatting with these men. They took life on the bounce and were always good company.

The grinding tug of brake shoes replaced the bark of the engine. Jerking gently, the train slowed, then stopped at a lighted platform. Holland and Adams pulled on gloves and rose.

"Bendy," said Holland. "Next stop, and you can go to bed, Mr. Jordan. If you hurry, you'll make it by one o'clock."

Marc grinned. He too rose and returned to his own seat. He was staring idly through the dirty window glass at the ordered confusion on the platform when the car door banged open and the raucous, rasping voice of a newsboy shattered the quiet.

"Extry! Extry! Read all about it! Extry!"

Flipping him a coin, Marc spread the paper on his knees. Clutching fingers stretched the sheets taut. The flesh along his spine tingled. He stared aghast at the splotches of black ink.

> *Girl kidnapped!—Calumet, June 17, 1948. Miss Miriam Porter, daughter of Donald Porter of Tenth Avenue, was feared kidnapped tonight when her parents informed police she had not returned from a music lesson and could not be located.*
>
> *Miss Porter left the Crescent Studios at eight o'clock as usual following her lesson. Her instructor reports that she seemed in no way upset. She told fellow students that she planned to go directly home.*
>
> *This is the second time tragedy has struck the Porter home in less than a month. Her sister,*

Dolly, was injured fatally in an auto-train accident on the eve of her wedding. No attempt has yet been made by the kidnapper to contact the distraught parents. Police report that every effort—

An agony of helpless frustration tearing at his heart, Marc read the story to the end. The paper slipped unheeded to the floor as the train jerked and pulled out of town.

The fifteen-minute ride to Calumet consumed a lifetime. Marc snatched his bag from the rack and lunged forward to the front end of the train. His impatience was almost unbearable. He wanted to get out and push.

He was standing on the bottom car step when the train slowed for Calumet. Hitting the platform on a run, he hurried through the waiting room and dropped his bag unceremoniously on the information desk.

"Watch this for me, Duke," he called.

With a curt apology, he crowded ahead of a man about to enter a cab, and slammed the door.

"Police headquarters! Fast!"

"Yes, sir."

Gears clashed and the cab dodged recklessly through a dribble of traffic. It slid to a stop before the Municipal Building. Marc handed a bill to the driver, ran to the entrance and mounted the steps to Anderson's office three at a time.

He found Anderson and Porter in the office when he burst through the door. His eyes darted from one to the other questioningly.

"Any news?" he demanded.

Anderson shook his head. "Nope. Not yet."

"What happened?"

"Read the papers?"

"Yes."

"You know as much as we do."

Porter flicked the ash from his cigar with the end of his little finger.

"Miriam hasn't gotten home," he said coolly. "Personally, I don't think it's much to worry about."

Marc regarded him with mute fascination. How could Porter be so calm, almost detached?

"If that's the case, if you aren't worried, why all the excitement?"

Porter smiled wryly. "Cynthia. She threw a fit. Her little chick's the apple of her eye."

"But what did happen?"

"I tell ya, Jordan," snapped Anderson, "we don't know. Miss Porter left the Crescent Studios at eight o'clock, 'n never got home. That's it."

"No word at all?"

"None."

"She'll turn up," said Porter. "Probably decided to go out with friends."

"What friends? Haven't you checked with them? Where's Tony?"

Porter hesitated. "Yes, we've been in touch with most of them. Doctor Bodine's at the house now with Cynthia."

"Karl Snyder's back in town. Did you reach him?"

"He's one that can't be located," grunted Anderson. "We're lookin' for him."

"You remember, Jerry," said Marc, his voice soft and crisp, "that I told you our troubles weren't over."

"Hang it all," growled Anderson, "I'm not clairvoyant. I can't furnish nursemaids for everybody in town."

"What do you plan to do?"

"What is there to do?" questioned Porter. "Suppose she's kidnapped, which I doubt, the next move's up to the kidnapper. In the meantime, we wait."

Some of the anger drained out of Marc, leaving him limp and weary. His mind told him they were right, though his heart yearned for action.

"You staying here, Don?" he asked.

Porter nodded. "Cynthia insisted. She made me come down to prod the cops. Not that anything I say could improve the efficiency of this office!"

Smiling in spite of himself, Marc turned slowly to the door. "Any objections if I go out to your house?"

The cigar in Porter's hand described circles in the air.

"Heck no!" he said. "Go ahead. Maybe you can talk some sense into Cynthia. I can't."

Leaving police headquarters, Marc strode to a drug store, hunting a phone. When there was no answer to his call, he thumbed through the phone book and made a second one.

An even voice came to him. "Hello."

"Thatcher, Jordan. Thought you were hired to watch the Porter family?"

"Uh-uh. Just the crown prince. Him and your crook friend."

"We should have watched Miriam. My stupidity. D'you have a string on Meegan?"

"Well," Thatcher's voice dropped, "fact is, Klutz lost him this evening. So far we haven't picked him up. I've got a man at his rooming house now, watching for him."

Marc's heart sank. "I knew it! I'd have bet a month's pay. Where's Klutz now?"

"Here. Just came in a few minutes ago."

"Don't let him move. Stay there. I want to talk to him."

Thatcher kept bachelor quarters in a large apartment house a few blocks from his office. In his business, the time by the clock meant nothing. He admitted that his best work was done at night.

Marc covered the distance to the apartment at a dog trot. Entering the unobtrusively elegant living room, he found Thatcher, resplendent in a purple bathrobe, stretched out on a leather divan smoking a cigarette in an amber holder. Opposite, perched nervously on the edge of a chair and twirling a hat in his fingers, sat Klutz. He was squat and powerful, slightly bowlegged.

Marc glared angrily at him. "Blast you, Mike!"

Klutz bristled. His thick eyebrows crowded together in a frown and he returned Marc's gaze.

"Now listen here," he said defensively, "don't climb my frame. I ain't got only one pair o' eyes, an' one pair o' legs. That goon's slick. He give me the slip."

Marc suppressed his wrath. Klutz was good, and he'd had a tough assignment.

"Okay, Mike, you couldn't help it. How'd he get away?"

"Smoothest dodge that's been pulled on me fer many a day. He moseys into Gander's department store—the big one on Main Street—'bout four-thirty. He monkeys around for thirty-forty minutes. He buys a pair o' stockings. Then he fumbles around the silk pants counter, looks at gloves, and drifts over to the jewelry counter. He had me 'bout nuts tryin' to keep busy and outa the road o' the floor walker.

"Jewelry's close t' the elevators. He waits till one of 'em's almost loaded. Quick like a bunny rabbit, he ducks in just before she takes off. Nothin' I could do except grab the next one, and pray. I don't pray good. I never seen him again. There's half a dozen ways o' gettin' outa that store."

"That," said Marc sadly, "is that." He turned to Thatcher. "What've you learned about Meegan?"

Fastidiously, Thatcher emptied the cigarette holder with thumb and forefinger. After cleaning it carefully, he slipped it into his pocket and clamped his hands behind his head before replying.

"Not much. Came here from Chicago a few months ago. Haven't had a report from my Chicago associates. He lives in a fourth-rate rookery on the East Side, hangs out at the Purple Pot."

"Who're his friends?"

"Don't seem to have many. A lone wolf. Only person he's been seen with is a beat up streetwalker, Trixie Donovan."

"Who's she? Have you checked her?"

Thatcher nodded. "Some. Born here in Calumet. She was in the movies for a while; played bit parts in the silents. When the movies got to talking, she couldn't get jobs. Been on the street ever since. She worked in Chicago a few years and came back here a short time ago. Haven't found out exactly when."

"Any idea what Meegan's up to?"

"Nope. One of my stools thinks he's on a job, but don't know what it is."

Marc grimaced. "I never thought about it, but I suppose you do have stool pigeons." He glanced at Klutz. "Has Meegan done anything suspicious since you've been watching him?"

"Not specially. Hangs around this Trixie dame, but I don't figger it's no love party. Last night, 'bout midnight, he moseyed by the Porters' and cut through the park. I seen him use one o' them little pencil flashlights in the bushes like he was huntin somethin'. Didn't take him long. He beat it right outa there."

"The park's directly opposite the Porters'," muttered Marc. "You couldn't see what he was doing?"

Klutz shook his head. "Nope. I'm across the street. Gotta keep back when there ain't people around. Mebbe that's when he spotted me, at that. I seen where he went but that's all."

Though he was outwardly calm, Marc's brain seethed with a jumble of conflicting thoughts. He stepped to a telephone on a stand at Thatcher's side, flipped the dial.

"Yeah?"

"Jordan. Jerry, were there any cars stolen tonight?"

"Hold it." There was a slight pause. "Yeah. Olds sedan. Snatched about supper time."

"Where was it taken from?"

"Parked across from Gander's. This dame went in to pay a bill, and in five minutes it was gone."

"You're looking for it?"

"Why, sure, you sap!"

"Look hard, Jerry. Very hard."

"Why? You onto something?"

"Clairvoyance," replied Marc dryly. "'Bye."

He hung up and crooked his finger at Klutz.

"Come with me, Mike. I'm headed for the Porters'. You'll be useful."

Klutz glanced inquiringly at Thatcher.

Thatcher waved indifferently. "Go ahead. You're working for him."

Together the two men left the apartment and walked to the corner of Main Street where Marc hailed a night owl cab. Relaxing wearily against the cold cushions, he packed and lit his pipe.

At the Porters', Marc paid the driver and stood irresolute at the curb.

"D'you have a light, Mike?" he said.

"Yeah." Klutz fished a flashlight from the pocket of his sagging topcoat.

"Show me where you saw Meegan hunt, last night."

Klutz led the way across the street to the park. He followed a narrow path through a thick border of shrubs. Fifteen feet or so from the street, he stopped beside a small, low tree.

"'Bout here, near's I can figger."

Marc took the light and played it around the base of the tree. He studied the smooth plane of closely matted leaves, concentrating on one spot where the surface was tumbled and broken.

Carefully, with the tips of his fingers, he brushed away the leaves, exposing to view a layer of fine, smooth loam. A long sigh whistled through his teeth. Klutz grunted with surprise.

"A rod!" he gasped.

Marc probed the spot with the finger of light. Clearly discernible in the soft dirt was the imprint of a gun. Instinctively, Marc slid his forefinger into his pocket and touched a small lump of lead.

"So. This is what our friend was doing. Wonder what calibre it was."

"Can't tell from only that print," said Klutz.

Marc shrugged. "Of course not. But I would like to know. This is most illuminating."

"What the devil'd he hide a rod there for?"

"So it wouldn't be found on him, naturally. That would've been embarrassing. Let's go."

They re-crossed the street and mounted the veranda steps. A pacing shadow momentarily darkened the window. Marc knocked, and then entered without waiting.

Fingers buried in his hair, Tony huddled on the davenport. He looked up slowly as they entered. Marc suppressed a gasp. Usually boyish and debonair, Tony's face was gray with strain. He seemed a tired old man.

Aloof, patently savoring the catastrophe, sat Sarah. Her head and her knitting needled synchronized with the steady beat of her rocking chair. Her spectacles triumphantly rode the end of her nose.

Cynthia's demeanor was most surprising. Expecting to find her again in hysterics, Marc was dumbfounded by her fury as she stalked about the room. Her eyes glittered and her lips were grim. She halted abruptly at his appearance, stared at him a moment, then continued her prowling.

"No news?" questioned Marc.

Cynthia shook her head.

"What makes you think she's—?"

"Kidnapped?" Cynthia snarled the word. "Because she's never gone out without telling me before. Never!"

"Could be a first time."

"Not Miriam. Not my baby."

"Where's Joel?"

"How should I know? I can't keep track of that fool. Hanging around some cheap woman, probably."

"Is there anything I can do to help?"

"Yes. Get out! Leave me alone!"

Frowning, Marc stood beside Tony and sympathetically laid a hand on his shoulder.

"Let's go home, Doc," he said softly.

Silently, Tony rose and plodded out. Marc rescued his own hat and Tony's from an end table and followed.

Still silent, Tony climbed into the driver's seat of his car. Klutz approached as Marc was about to follow.

"How about me, Mr. Jordan?"

Marc started. He'd forgotten Klutz. "Any idea where you might find Meegan?"

Klutz shrugged. "Usually he's at the Purple Pot."

"Hunt for him. If you don't have any luck, come back here. Watch this house the rest of the night. Hop in. We'll take you to town."

When they had discharged Klutz at a cab stand, Marc heaved a weary sigh.

"I need a drink."

"God, so do I!" These, Tony's first words, were barely whispered. He wheeled the car into a vacant space beside a tavern. Entering a booth, they ordered and silently waited delivery.

Tony's hand shook as he raised his glass, drained it at a gulp and waved for a refill before the waiter had time to turn away.

"I wonder where she is," he muttered.

Marc pulled his pipe from his pocket, glared at it distastefully, and shoved it back. He emptied his glass and also ordered another.

"Do you suppose she's hurt? Maybe dead? Marc, do you think she's dead? Marc, do you?" His voice rose until it cracked.

"How I wish I knew," replied Marc fervently. "I think— Tony, I don't think she's dead or hurt. There's something peculiar about Cynthia. She should be hysterical with grief, and she's not. I don't know—"

Tony's eyes commenced to glaze. He picked up a dinner knife and, holding it like a dagger, viciously stabbed the table top. He raised the knife in mid-air, his teeth gleaming through tight drawn lips.

"If I find someone's mistreated Miriam, I'll—!"

Impulsively, Marc reached across the table and gripped his arm.

"Easy, my boy," he said soothingly. "Relax. Won't do her any good for you to crack."

Tony threw the knife on the table and again drained his glass.

8

Marc slept little that night. His bed seemed full of cinders. Tossing and twisting, he whipped it into a tangle. When, toward morning, he dozed, his mind was filled with the zing of bullets. Duck and dodge as he might, they thudded into his body, but to his overwhelming bewilderment, caused no pain.

When the silhouette of trees outside his window became more clearly etched against a brightening sky, Marc tumbled the bedclothes to the floor and slowly dressed. Glancing compassionately at Tony, he drew a pitcher of water and set it with a glass on his bed table, then walked slowly to the street.

He breathed great gasps of the nippy air, and set off with long, even strides. Almost unconsciously, his feet led him to the residential district. The sun was tilting golden fingers through the trees when he reached the park opposite the Porter house.

Slowly, he walked along a shrub-lined path. The happy chatter of the birds seemed far removed from human terror. Stopping a few feet from the street, his mouth twitched at the sight of Klutz huddled in a woebegone knot on a bench.

"Morning, Klutz," he said.

Klutz shuddered and stiffly straightened up.

"Oh. Howdy, Mr. Jordan."

"Any excitement?"

"Nope." Klutz shook his head. "Nary a thing."

"I gather you didn't find Meegan."

"You gather right. I didn't."

Marc continued to the street. He looked thoughtfully at the silent house. Passing along the side street, he circled the block, then headed back toward town.

The early birds were out busily selecting the fat worms when he got to the business district. Suddenly feeling the pangs of hunger, he stopped at a lunch counter and wolfed a hurried breakfast.

When he once more joined the growing bustle on the sidewalk he felt better. Full of new confidence, he set off with a firm step toward the Municipal Building.

"Anderson in?" he asked of the desk man.

"He was, Mr. Jordan. Went out to eat. Oughta be back any minute."

"I'll wait in his office," he said, mounting the steps.

The door to Anderson's office stood ajar. Marc entered, ensconced himself in his usual chair with his feet on the desk, and set to work tuning up his pipe. He had a good glow going when Anderson stamped in.

"Blast you, Jordan! You and your alley cat manners. Get your feet off my desk."

"Good morning, Jerry. Sorry. I think better this way."

"What you got to think about, this time o' day?"

"Good question. Any more questions?"

"Yeah. What're you doin' here so chipper, so early?"

"Any news on the Porter case?"

"No. I'll call Porter. Maybe they've heard somethin'." He reached for the phone. As he picked it up, the bell jangled.

"Yeah? . . . Yeah? . . . Well, I'll be— All right, thanks."

Anderson returned the phone to its cradle and wheeled about, a quizzical glitter in his pop eyes.

"There," he said dryly, "is your case."

"What do you mean?"

"Miss Porter was picked up this morning—drunk! Some guy on the South Side found her settin' on his doorstep. She's at St. Lukes' Hospital."

"Hospital?" Marc thumped his feet on the floor. "Why wasn't she taken home?"

"Seems she was also sick."

"Okay. Let's go." Marc stood up and knocked his pipe against the heel of his hand.

"Go where?"

"Aren't you going to the hospital to see her?"

"Me? I'll say not! I ain't got time to run after drunk dames."

"But, Jerry—"

"Now listen to me, Jordan." Anderson shook a stumpy finger at Marc. "You're wastin' my time. You tell your fancy friends to quit botherin' me. I'm a busy man."

Marc shrugged. "You're making a mistake, Jerry. A serious one."

Anderson snorted. "So it's a mistake. I've made 'em before and I'll make 'em again. But I'll take the chance!"

Stopping at the door, Marc hesitated, started to speak, then changed his mind. He hurried from the building and waved imperiously to a passing cab.

At the hospital, he glanced questioningly at the little woman who, with prim efficiency, reigned at the reception desk.

"Good morning," he said. "I understand Miss Miriam Porter was admitted this morning. Is that right?"

A carefully manicured fingernail slid down a book file, flipped out a card.

"Miss Porter—yes, sir. She was brought in a short time ago."

"May I see her?"

The receptionist hesitated. "I'm afraid not, sir. Visiting hours are two to four."

"I see. This is a rather unusual case. I'm Miss Porter's attorney, and very anxious to see her. Could it be arranged?"

"Well," she replied, "perhaps. If you'll be seated, sir, I'll call the house physician."

Marc squatted on the edge of a stiff chair in the corner of the lobby and twirled his hat in his fingers. Through a door opposite he could see the snowy glint of uniformed nurses gliding by. He checked off each of twenty-five minutes on the hands of a large clock before a small, wizened, white-coated man with a stethoscope looped around his neck approached.

"I'm Doctor Mathews. Mr.—?"

"Jordan."

"Mr. Jordan. Miss Cleves tells me you wish to see Miss Porter. Her attorney, I believe."

"Yes."

"I see. It's rather unusual. Our rules, you know."

"Doctor, have you notified her family that she's here?"

"Yes. She was admitted in an intoxicated condition. I first presumed it would be a case for the police. However, I am perhaps in error."

"Just plain drunk, huh?"

Doctor Mathews pursed his lips and tapped them with his spectacles. "Yes and no. She undoubtedly had partaken of a considerable concentration of alcoholic beverage. However, there are signs that she may have had something slightly more potent; one of the sleep-inducing drugs, perhaps. I haven't examined her carefully, and she does seem to be rallying rather quickly."

"Drugged!" breathed Marc. "Where is she?"

"In the emergency ward."

Marc assumed a disinterested, professional air he was far from feeling.

"As her attorney, Doctor Mathews, may I make a request? First, will you move her immediately to a private room?"

"That, I believe, could be arranged."

"Second, will you examine her, carefully and at once, for evidence of drugs and any other mistreatment?"

His lips still pursed, Doctor Mathews regarded Marc quizzically.

"Young man, may I ask why you are so concerned?"

"You may," replied Marc tersely. "Did you know, Doctor, that Miss Porter disappeared early last evening, and that her family feared she'd been kidnapped?"

The doctor's eyebrows arched, and he clucked with surprise.

"Indeed! No, I was not aware of that circumstance. It places a somewhat different complexion on the case."

"Doesn't it," said Marc dryly. "Will you see that she's taken care of?"

"I will attend to it at once."

"Thanks. Furthermore, I'd like to see her at the earliest possible moment."

"There won't be any difficulty about that. As soon as she has been moved, and I've made my examination, I will send for you."

Doctor Mathews trotted off and disappeared into the cavernous corridor. Marc fired his pipe to help pass the time.

The pipe was emptied, refilled, and emptied again before Doctor Mathews peeked around the door and gestured to him. Marc rose quickly and followed.

He was led to an austere but airy corner room on the second floor. Miriam, pale and limp, lay on her side with her face away from the light. She gave Marc a languid glance, without moving her head. He sank on a chair beside her and pressed her fingers.

"Hi, Mimi. Glad to see you," he said fervently.

A wisp of a smile flitted across her colorless lips.

"I'm glad too, Marc," she whispered.

"How is she, Doc?"

"Fine. A few hours' rest and she will be up and about."

Marc's eyes searched the doctor's questioningly. "There's no—that is, has she been—?"

The doctor shook his head vigorously.

"All right to question her?" continued Marc.

"Surely. Just don't stay too long," he replied, slipping quietly out the door.

"What happened, Miriam? Will it tire you to talk?" She shook her head almost imperceptibly. "I'm limp as a wet dish rag and sort of sick. But I'll be all right."

"What did happen?"

"I don't know, exactly. It happened so quickly."

"Where were you?"

"Walking home from the Crescent Studios. It was dark, about eight-thirty. A man pounced on me from the bushes along the walk in the park."

"One man?"

"To be truthful, Marc, I don't know whether it was one or six. I didn't see anyone. The first thing I knew, a heavy sack was pulled over my head. I almost smothered! The cloth smelled like ether. The bottom of the sack was jerked tight and pinned my arms. I couldn't move, and I could hardly breathe. I was picked up and shoved into a car. I think there was only one person, and it must have been a man, because I was pushed in, the door was slammed, the front door opened, and the engine started. If there had been more than one, the first man would have gotten in with me."

"Did you see the car?"

Miriam shook her head. "There are bushes on both sides of the sidewalk there. You can't see the street. He jumped on me right where one of the park walls comes out. His car must've been parked back far enough so that I couldn't see it."

"You're not much help, Miriam. Then what happened?"

"I must've passed out. I don't know how long it was before I came to. 1 was sitting in the car, or a car. My hands and feet were tied, and there was a rag tied through my mouth. Oh, Marc, it was terrible! It's like a hideous nightmare!" Miriam whimpered softly.

Marc stroked her hair gently. "Easy, Miriam. It could've been lots worse. How long were you there?"

Miriam's body shook with a convulsive shudder. She dabbed at her eyes with a piece of cleansing tissue and smiled wanly.

"Give me a drink, Marc. My mouth tastes like used flypaper."

Marc poured her a glass of water and held her head while she sipped it slowly.

"My mind's almost blank. It's like a dream. It was dark, pitch dark. Someone was sitting in the front seat. I could hear breathing and see the glow of a cigarette. I must've gasped or gurgled or something. Anyway, he snapped at me, 'Shut up, sister! Keep quiet and you won't get hurt.' I kept quiet."

"You poor kid!"

"After a while I got the courage to grunt some more. That gag almost drove me crazy. I wanted to get it out more than I've ever wanted anything in my life. After a while he came into the back seat and untied the cloth. Before he took it out, he said, 'Make a sound, baby, and I'll beat you over the head. That's a promise.' Then he took it out. What a relief! That was the worst part of the whole thing. The rag must've been soaked in glue!"

Miriam paused and sighed wearily. Marc rose and slow-ly walked to the window and back.

"Go on," he said.

"That's about all, Marc. I asked for a drink. I meant a drink of water, but he brought me a glass of whisky. It tast-ed awful, but I drank it. I needed it. After that I must've passed out again, because I don't remember a thing except waking up sitting on someone's doorstep."

"No idea how or when you got there?"

She shook her head. "None."

Marc thrust his hands deep in his pockets and studied her. Miriam's frank eyes were black-rimmed, her face pale, and her lips parched and cracked, She couldn't be dissem-bling, or could she?

"You never got a look at your assailant?"

"No."

"Would you recognize his voice?"

She shrugged. "Maybe. I dread going to sleep for fear I'll hear it!"

"Then it wasn't someone whose voice you did know?"

She didn't speak for several minutes. Then she said slowly, "I can't explain it, Marc, but I've a feeling that I've heard that voice before."

"Where? When?"

"I haven't the slightest idea. I've tried and tried to think, but I can't."

"Damn!" Marc paced to the window and stared unsee-ingly into the street. He was relieved when, on turning back to the bed, he saw some color in Miriam's cheeks and a faint grin twitching her lips.

"Herewith, my application for a job as a sleuth, Marc. I did something that may further the cause of justice."

"What?"

"When friend kidnapper loosened my hands to give me a drink, I unfastened my monogram pin and slipped it be-hind the cushions."

"Miriam!" Marc strode to her, patted her shoulder and solemnly shook her hand. "You smart little devil! Maybe that'll tag our man, if we can find the car."

"So I thought."

"An inspiration! This is information for Anderson." Marc hurried to the door. "So long, kid. Take it easy. Your family should soon be here."

"Thanks, Marc, I will."

Marc hurried from the hospital. As he trotted down the steps, a taxi slithered up to the curb and stopped with a jerk. An unshaven, harassed man tumbled out, followed by a very imminently expectant mother. Full of solicitous worry, the man helped her as she awkwardly, painfully climbed the steps. Marc couldn't help a sympathetic smile.

He climbed into the recently vacated cab. The driver sagged limply behind the wheel and mopped his face with a big handkerchief.

"Wow!" he gasped. "Brother, am I glad to get rid o' that fare!"

"A close call?"

"Close! Been any closer'n my cab'd of been a maternity ward."

"At least you'd get your name in the papers."

"No, thanks. Where to, Mac?"

"Police headquarters."

"Yes, *sir.*"

Anderson was polishing his thick glasses. He peered myopically at Marc, popped his glasses into place and grunted.

"Oh. You again."

"I just left Miss Porter, Jerry. She was not drunk."

"Not drunk?"

"Not drunk. Doped. Kidnapped and doped."

"Huh?"

"You heard. She was smothered in a sack soaked in ether, kidnapped, and then given a Mickey."

"You kidding?"

Exasperation drove blood to Marc's temples.

"Why should I?" he snapped.

Anderson shrugged. "How should I know?" He ogled Marc craftily. "How do you know she was drugged? How do you know she ain't puttin' on a act to cover a big night out?"

Marc hesitated. "That occurred to me, but I don't think so. I know Miriam. In the first place, I don't think she's the type, and in the second place, I don't think she could put on that kind of an act."

Anderson chuckled. "These dames'll fool you, my boy. You get a little older and you'll find that out."

Angry, and also a little uncertain, Marc stared at Anderson. His confused thoughts were interrupted by a bang on the door, and a cop entered.

"Turned up that car that was swiped last night, boss. It's out in the lot."

Marc wheeled to him. "An Olds sedan?"

The officer nodded. "Yup. That's right."

"Did you get the driver?"

"Nope. Parked the car in front of Gander's store and ducked in. Time I got there, he was gone."

"That store's becoming a regular crooks' run," muttered Marc. "How'd you happen to find the car?"

"Spotted the license number when he went by my corner. I whistled. He didn't stop, so I took after him."

"What'd he look like?"

"Couldn't tell much. Short, stocky feller."

Marc turned to Anderson. "Jerry, may I try an experiment?"

Anderson returned Marc's stare. "Depends. What is it?"

"Officer," continued Marc, "will you go to that car and look behind the cushion of the back seat? Bring up anything you find."

The officer's jaw sagged with surprise. He turned questioningly to Anderson.

"Go ahead," said Anderson with a wave of his hand. "Let's play games."

Marc judiciously measured out a pipe full of tobacco and carefully tamped it in place. He had smoke curling from his pipe when the cop returned.

"A pin," he said, staring at the object in his palm. "A pin with the initial 'M.'"

9

"Strike! Nice work, Tony. We've got 'em on the run."

Tony, his tie askew and his cherubic face beaded with perspiration, turned from the foul line with a contented grin.

"Can't miss tonight, Marcus. One beer says I beat you twenty pins."

"One beer it is," chuckled Marc.

"Go get 'em. This Lions gang is hot, too. Maybe we need some pins."

A stocky man squeezed into the narrow space beside Tony.

"What's got into you guys?" he asked plaintively. "Go easy, will ya? We need a game."

Tony laughed. "So do we, George. Watch our anchor man, Mr. Jordan. Know him?" He pointed to Marc, who was selecting a ball from the rack.

"Best money bowler in the league. Never could figger how he makes them long feet and knock knees track."

"He's a symphony of awkward grace," said Tony affectionately. "Quite a guy. Atta boy, Marc," he called as Marc, with three careful steps and an easy swing, angled the ball down the alley and swept the pins away as with a broom.

His turn to grin. Marc glanced at the score sheet.

"All even," he said. "You'll have to strike out to beat me. Another beer says you can't."

"Taken. You watch."

They waited amid the slamming rumble of balls and pins while the other contestants took their turn. Tony stamped to the rack, rubbed his hand on the dirty towel tied to the post, and fondled the chalk block. Taking careful aim, he slid the ball down the center for a strike. Mockingly, he held up one finger. Repeating with towel and chalk, he rolled a second strike, and held up two fingers. His third took nine pins.

He did a tripping toe dance back to the bench and rumpled Marc's hair.

"Let's see the maestro beat that," he said.

Marc smiled ruefully. "Tough, but I can try." He sighted across his ball, and rolled a perfect split.

Tony hooted. "Oh my! That's too bad," he said with mock sympathy. "You was robbed."

Marc bounced his final ball down the alley and turned away, rolling down his sleeves.

"We take the game, and you win the beer, you thief," he said as they huddled around the score board.

"Roll one for fun?" questioned Tony.

Marc shook his head. "Not tonight."

They paid for the games, and walked across the street to a tavern.

"How about something heavier than beer, since you pay?" asked Tony.

"Beer or nothing," replied Marc.

Tony studied his friend's lean, sober face.

"Exercising that will power, eh?"

With a level stare, Marc returned his glance. "Right. And yours. Next time you get stinko, I'll leave you in the gutter to rot."

"Not a bad idea. Comfortable spot, the gutter. Okay. Beer it is."

They sipped from their glasses in silence for several minutes. Marc, tamping his pipe, shot a glance at Tony.

"Seen Miriam?" he asked.

The boyish exuberance slipped from Tony like a mask. He nodded.

"Last night. I stopped in for a few minutes. She's had a tough time, but she seemed all right."

"Was she doped?"

"No doubt about it. Ether, and then a mild Mickey. No harm done, though."

Marc ran his fingers through his unruly hair. "I wonder why. I don't understand it."

A surge of rage swelled in Tony's chest. He twirled his glass in the puddle of water on the table and then glanced at Marc.

"If I ever get my hands on the whelp who manhandled her, I'll kill him! I'll twist his neck until his head snaps off!"

"Easy, Tony," cautioned Marc gently. "Don't talk that way. It could get you in real trouble. Let's run this down in an orderly fashion."

Tony couldn't suppress the snarl in his voice.

"Orderly nothing! It's time for action. Miriam's sister's dead. She's been shot at, and kidnaped. What the devil goes on?"

Marc shrugged wearily. "I wish I knew."

"I wish you'd tell me what you do know!"

"I know very little, Tony. Something evil and vicious goes on. Take Miriam's ordeal. A kidnapee is usually held for ransom. Yet no effort was made to contact her parents. She was held all night and released unharmed, except for rough handling and a little dope. Two days, and no word from her kidnaper. Why?"

Tony dropped his head on his arms. "You're right as usual," he said, straightening. "It's fishy. But if I ever find out who—"

"Don't do anything rash. You may be needed before this stinking affair is over."

They finished their beer in silence.

"Let's go," said Marc briskly. "I've work to do at the office. Been neglecting my job lately."

He paid the check and they returned to the street.

"So you're going to slave," said Tony. "Not me. See you later."

He waved as they separated.

Poor Tony. Marc watched him plod up the street and climb into his car.

Walking in the opposite direction to where his own car was parked, he climbed in and drove into the thin trickle of late traffic.

At an intersection several blocks from the bowling alley, a green traffic light suddenly flashed red, and continued to flash. A klaxon mounted on a pole shouted a raucous warning. Marc drew over to the curb and stopped. A fire truck rumbled by, with a roar and wail to startle the dead. In a few seconds another smaller truck followed. The klaxon coughed into silence, the siren wail died to a whisper, and the traffic light resumed its phlegmatic cycle.

A fire runner from early youth, Marc was tempted to follow. But a picture of his desk, piled high with neglected and unfinished business, flashed across his mind, and he continued on his way.

He parked at the railroad building, methodically locked his car, and headed for the entrance. The night operator grinned a greeting.

"Evenin', Mr. Jordan. You gonna work? Ain't you got no sense?"

Marc smiled. "Guess not, Joe."

"Where's the fire? Just heared the enjynes go by."

"I don't know. I nearly followed the trucks, but my will power won out."

"I like a good fire," said Joe wistfully. "Wisht I'd a been a fireman, 'stead of a elevator jockey."

"So do I," replied Marc fervently. "Then we could pour water on other people's troubles, and let it go at that."

"Yeah," said Joe with a puzzled look at him. "Don't work too late, Mr. Jordan."

Marc snapped on the light in the quiet office, hung his hat and coat on the rack, and looked out over the sleeping city. His glance spanned the railroad yard dotted with winking, colored lights to where, in the near distance, a red glow etched the silhouette of a building. Fascinated, Marc watched. Suddenly, with a puff of crimson, the glow increased, died, and grew again.

Forgetting his good intentions, Marc snatched his hat and coat and with swift steps strode back to the elevator.

Joe, answering his insistent signal, stared in astonishment.

"Short night's work, Mr. Jordan," he said.

Marc grimaced. "Looks like a nice fire across town. My will power's all shot."

"Gees! Wisht I could go along," Joe said enviously.

Leaving the building on a run, Marc started his car with a jerk, executed an illegal U turn and headed at racing speed toward the fire.

He tried to guess what was burning. From the direction, it might be one of the small manufacturing plants that huddled in the borderline area between the business and residential districts. The building in line with the fire was a grain elevator. Maybe that was it! Or the lumber yard beyond. Both had beautiful possibilities.

His pulse throbbed with excitement as he toyed with death and the law. He passed the grain elevator reaching skyward in majestic silence. The lumber yard, in the next block, was likewise dark and deserted. A short distance farther and the buildings decreased in height, fanned away from the street. Here the red glow was plainly visible.

A gasp whistled through his lips. The fire showed angry and voracious through the trees of the park. The Porter place!

Marc left his car and ran through the park. Tingling excitement was replaced by horror. He pushed through the ring of morbidly curious spectators who stared at the holocaust.

The Porter yard was confusion incarnate. The garage, almost half the size of the house and set a few feet from it, was completely engulfed in curling fingers of flame. The masonry walls made a retort, and fire billowed through the roof like a Bessemer converter. Through one burned out door, Marc could see the ghostly outline of a car. Suddenly the din of hoarse voices and the slap and sizzle of water was punctured by a thud. The flaming car bounced under the impetus of an exploding gas tank. Streamers of fire sprayed into the drive.

The house was a blaze of light. Firemen played heavy sprays from front and rear on the side near the garage, and over the roof. Others drenched the garage itself with little visible effect. Circling around the yard, Marc could see that, except for blistered paint, some cracked glass and charred eaves, the house was undamaged.

At one side, gazing at the inferno in mute, stunned, unbelieving terror, stood Miriam, her arm around her mother. Cynthia, her hair in braids and clutching a bathrobe to her throat, clung to her daughter. Their faces were pink masks.

"Are you all right?" asked Marc anxiously.

Miriam turned to him. Her pert hat and light coat seemed ridiculously incongruous.

"Oh, Marc," she gasped. "Yes, we're all right."

"What happened?"

Miriam shook her head. "I don't know. It started before I got here."

"Anyone hurt?"

"No. The Harrisons are heroes. They're moving things away from the garage side. Tony's helping. I'm glad you're here."

"Why?"

"Just glad."

"Where's your father?"

"He hasn't come home from the club yet."

"Maybe I can help."

Marc started across the lawn to be met by a policeman who raised a restraining hand.

"Where ya think yer goin', bud?" he growled.

"To see if I can help, Charlie."

"Oh. Hello, Mr. Jordan. Okay. Be careful. Helluva lot of gasoline in that garage. Don't get too close."

Marc skirted the yard and climbed onto the veranda from the far end. In spite of a light breeze which blew some of the smoke and blistering heat away from the house, he gasped and choked as he groped through the door. He bumped into Harrison, who was trundling a table across the hall.

"Grab the rug, Marc. Roll it away from the fire." Tony emerged from the haze, disheveled and red-eyed, carrying an armful of lamps.

Marc leaped to obey. Water from the protecting hoses splashed and dripped through the broken windows. Billows of smoke hampered him, but he succeeded in rolling the rug against the far wall. Noting that this cleared the room, he bounded up the stairs.

On the top step squatted Mrs. Harrison, one arm clutching a stair post and the other pressing a towel to her face.

"Tony," shouted Marc, "up here. Quick!"

In an instant Tony joined him.

"Let's get her out of here."

They made a chair of their arms and picked up the frail form. Harrison met them at the bottom of the stairs.

"Get an armful of blankets, Harrison," ordered Marc.

Carrying Mrs. Harrison to a far corner of the lawn, they made a bed of blankets, stretched her out and covered her. Shocked and incoherent, Miriam dropped to her knees beside her.

"Oh, Dudy! I'm sorry. I shouldn't have let you go in."

Mrs. Harrison coughed and smiled wanly. "I'm all right, Miss Miriam. The smoke kinda got me!"

Marc's mouth twitched. "Poetic understatement!"

"Sure you're all right, Dudy?"

"Sure." She breathed in deeply. "My, that air tastes good."

Marc turned to Tony. "How're things inside?"

Tony mopped his teary, smoke-blackened eyes. "Okay, I think. All the rooms on the garage side are cleared. 'Bout all we can do."

"How'd you happen to be here?"

Tony shot a red-eyed glance at Marc. "Oh," he replied, looking back at the fire, "I just happened by."

Marc studied him in silence for a moment. Then, noting that Mrs. Harrison was recuperating under Miriam's care, he walked away, slowly skirting the crowd. Arriving at the rear of the house, he approached a white-slickered fireman who stood at one side.

"Nice bonfire, Ted."

The firemen glanced at Marc. He jettisoned a mouthful of tobacco juice before replying.

"Beaut, for a little one," he said with professional calm. "Put yer line on the house, boys," he called to one of the hose crews. "Let the garage burn."

Turning back to Marc, he continued in a matter of fact voice, "Nothin' to do with that garage but let her burn."

"Know how it started?"

Ted shook his head. "How do any of 'em start? Carelessness, I reckon."

"I've run to lots of fires, but I never saw one burn like that."

Ted snorted with disgust. "Place's full o' inflammables. Understand there's twenty-thirty gallons o' oil, lotta paint and varnish, and two hundred gallons o' gas in there! Damfools! Just luck it didn't blow the house down too."

"Can you save the house?"

"Sure. Got'er stopped there. Might's well let the rest go. Total loss anyhow. That's gas there." He pointed to the far corner where white hot flames roared to the sky as fiercely as ever. "Every time we hit that corner with a hose, she spreads worse. Oh, we could smother it with chemicals, but what fer? Just have raw gas on our hands to worry about. Better to let 'er burn and git it over with."

"I don't understand."

"Look," said Ted patiently. "There's a lotta gas in there. All right. So we smother it. Then what? Coupla hours from now a spark hits and—poof! Got the job to do over. This way, when she's out, she's out."

"Good logic. You know your business."

Ted spat. "Sure oughta."

They watched the fire in silence. The gabled roof was gone completely, leaving only a masonry shell. The flames died to a smoldering flicker except for the gasoline-fed blow torch in the corner which continued unabated. At Ted's orders the hose lines were shut off, until only one remained to spray the house.

Marc wandered around the edge of the yard. Suddenly he darted into the thinning crowd and grabbed a thick-set man by the shoulder.

"Klutz!" he snapped. "What're you doing here?"

Klutz winced under the onslaught and looked up at Marc. He stuttered with surprise.

"Well, I seen the fire an'—"

"Why aren't you tending to business?" Marc pushed him into the shadows away from the crowd and possible prying ears.

"I am. I'm workin' on Meegan. He's around here somewheres."

"Don't you know where?"

Klutz hesitated. "Not exactly. I lost him a coupla hours ago, over in the park. I'm beatin' around huntin' fer him when this here fire busts out."

"Maybe he's in the crowd. Have you looked?"

"Yeah. Ain't seen him. If he's here, he's keepin' outa sight."

"Blast you, Klutz. It was to guard against something like this that you were hired. You snafued the job."

"Listen, Mr. Jordan"—Klutz bristled with indignation—"this guy's slick. Toughest goon to tail I ever worked on. I done the best I could."

Marc frowned. Some of his dread, forgotten in the excitement, returned.

10

Dressing quietly the next morning to avoid disturbing Tony, Marc sniffed his coat distastefully, and dropped it in a heap. He couldn't go about smelling like a bonfire. He selected other clothes and finished dressing, then slipped softly out of the apartment.

His desk was still piled high with paper work. Listlessly, he thumbed through several files. A case of disputed right of way had little appeal. Likewise the question of who should pay for a proposed pole line change. He pitched the papers into a drawer with disgust, propped his feet on the window ledge and meticulously cleaned his pipe.

He watched an engine puff importantly about the yard. The sleek Super Streak passenger run slid smoothly into sight around a bump in a hill, and stopped at the station. His eyes drifted across the staggering roof tops to the gray bulk of the grain elevator, and beyond to the smooth carpet of trees that sheltered many comfortable homes. Comfortable from without; strife-ridden within.

Stifled by the thought of routine, he clapped on his hat and abruptly left the office. Driving to the Porter house had become almost a habit, in which he again indulged this morning.

Already the yard, littered with debris and tramped to a paste, bustled with activity. Laborers drafted from

the brass factory were clearing the soggy mess that had
once been a garage. The skeleton of Miriam's car had been
dragged to one side and the workmen were piling charred
refuse into a truck.

Every window and door in the house stood open. Miriam, with the help of Mrs. Harrison who had apparently
recovered from her smoke bath, was hanging blankets,
linen and clothes out to air. Porter, a cigar wedged into
the corner of his mouth, stared at the havoc.

"Housecleaning, Don?" asked Marc quietly.

Porter jerked a glance at him. His voice was a snarl.

"Yeah! Going to change things around a little."

"Your garage does need some paint."

"Think so? One or two coats?"

"Didn't see you last night. You missed some delightful
excitement."

"Uh huh. I was delayed."

"How'd this grass fire get started, Don? Any idea?"

Fiercely Porter bounced the cigar across his mouth and
shook his head.

"Nope. Might've been a short circuit in the wiring. I
had some temporary stuff on my work bench."

"Will you rebuild?"

"Dunno yet. I suppose so. First thing to do is clean up
the mess."

Marc strolled closer to the wreckage. It reeked with the
dank odor of charred and water-soaked wood, mixed with
the smell of scorched oil. Several inches of evil-looking
water sloshed around a low spot in the concrete floor. The
thick masonry walls remained, but all inflammable material had been consumed.

Realizing that his presence hindered the workmen,
Marc wandered around to the back and peered curiously
through a small door.

In the far corner stood a brick partition, forming a cubicle four feet wide and about six feet deep. Steel cross pieces, several feet above the floor, carried a gasoline tank. The sides of the tank were bulged and twisted, and the blown out end exposed the blackened interior.

Along the bottom of the partition alternate bricks had been omitted for drainage, so that the floor could be flushed with a hose. These openings were now plugged at the bottom, and water several inches deep stood in the cubicle.

Below the gas tank stood a slatted steel rack on which Porter was accustomed to store oil and junk. The rack caught Marc's eye and engendered a puzzled frown. Gingerly he picked his way along the back wall.

He squinted at the rack. It was here that the fire had burned so fiercely and was still burning when he had left the night before. Oil drums, lying flat, were ranged along each side of the rack, leaving the center clear. In the middle of the rack lay a number of ash- covered strips of metal a half-inch wide and a foot long. They were pitted and limp, completely annealed by the blistering heat.

Picking up several strips, Marc wiped away the grime and studied them critically. His thoughts were punctured suddenly by a piercing shriek. Startled, he leaped to the door. Miriam stood rigidly immobile in a corner of the yard, one hand pressed to her lips, and stared into the bushes.

Marc and Porter reached her side simultaneously. She pointed to the base of a large shrub.

"Rags!" she exclaimed.

Wedged against the fence, his body bloated, his lips curled back to disclose gleaming fangs, and his head doubled under his fore paws, lay the body of Rags.

The trio stared at the dog. Stuffing the strips of metal into his pocket, Marc wormed his way through the foliage and dragged the carcass onto the grass. It rolled on its back, legs protruding stiffly, and seemed to stare at them reproachfully.

"Poisoned," said Marc tersely.

"Poisoned?" snapped Porter. "What the devil! Who'd poison old Rags?"

"Who indeed? More important, why?"

"Poor Rags," murmured Miriam.

"Was he all right last night?" asked Marc.

Miriam frowned. "He was with us at dinner, as usual, but I didn't see him after that."

"How about you, Don? Did you see him later?"

Porter shook his head. "Not after dinner."

"Harrison always fed him," said Miriam. "Ask him. He might know."

Marc turned Rags over with his foot and studied him for several minutes. Then he slowly crossed the yard to where a kennel stood guard at the rear gate. He surveyed the ground around the kennel; then squatting on hands and knees, he peered into the gloomy interior. A scrap of paper caught his eye, a piece of wax paper, smeared with bits of ground meat. Gingerly, Marc picked it up and sniffed it.

He rose and walked around the house to where Harrison was scrubbing the porch with broom and garden hose.

"Harrison, when did you see Rags last?"

Puzzled, Harrison leaned on the broom and stared at Marc.

"Last night, sir, when I fed him about eight o'clock."

"What did you feed him?"

"Dinner scraps, sir. Meat and potatoes."

"Did you give him any ground meat?"

"No sir."

"Do you ever feed him ground meat?"

"Very seldom, sir, unless the family is away and I have to buy something for him."

"Then you didn't give him this?"

Harrison glanced at the paper and shook his head.

"No sir."

"Did you see him this morning?"

"No sir. He wasn't in his kennel but I was so busy I didn't think much of it. Anything wrong?"

Marc nodded briefly. "With Rags. He's dead. Poisoned."

"My, my," gasped Harrison. "What next?"

Porter strode around the corner of the house.

"Find anything, Marc?"

Marc showed him the paper. "This. It was a packet of ground meat. Harrison says he didn't give it to Rags."

"Then whoever gave him the meat poisoned him."

"Could be."

Marc found a newspaper tucked between the pickets of the porch, tore a piece from it and wrapped the meat container. This he tucked into his pocket.

"I'll have it analyzed."

Abruptly he wheeled away and returned to the garage. As he approached the door, rubber-booted workmen splashed through the water, seized the oil rack and dragged it out of the cubicle. Angle iron feet screeched on the concrete and sliced through the barrier at the entrance. With a gurgle, the slimy water drained out. The men picked up the rack and tossed it onto the truck.

Puzzled, Marc was only half conscious of watching a laborer probe the center of the floor searching for the sewer drain. Finally he pulled up the bell trap cover. The water stood as before. Probing further, and then reaching into the drain, he pulled out a wad of rags. Immediately, with a rush, the water drained away and in a few seconds the floor was rid of the standing puddle.

The implication of the simple drama made Marc gasp. The sewer had been plugged! He darted back to the cubicle and examined the barrier across the entrance and the openings at the base of the partition. He dug his finger into one and turned up mud. He glanced up to find. Porter standing in the driveway.

"Don," he called, "does Harrison take care of your cars?"

"Yup."

"Wash them, grease them and so forth?"

"Yup."

"When was the last time one of your cars was washed?"

"Yesterday. He scrubbed mine."

"I see. Don't suppose he mentioned any trouble about water standing on the floor?"

"No. Why? Should he have?"

Marc shrugged away the question and glared angrily at the cubicle.

"How much gasoline did you have here?"

"Over two hundred gallons. The tank was nearly full."

"Dangerous fluid to have about. Someone might get hurt!"

"You're telling me, huh?"

Marc scraped his toe through the debris buried in the mud. A rectangular lump turned up and distastefully he rescued it from the muck. Fishing his knife from his pocket, he scraped away the charred exterior. Searching further, he exposed a second similar rectangle. Holding them between thumb and forefinger, he joined Porter.

"Whatcha got, Marc? Souvenirs?" Porter's tone was derisive.

"Souvenirs? Perhaps. Know what they are?"

"Sure," chuckled Porter. "Coupla chunks of charcoal."

"Yes. See you later, Don."

Marc salvaged the remains of the torn newspaper, wrapped his souvenirs, wiped his hands and left.

A few minutes later, still scowling, he found Doctor Lindstrom in his office chatting affably with a pert nurse. The doctor grinned as Marc entered.

"Sorry, Marcus. No golf. I've an appendix to work on, and a couple of well heeled ladies with water on the knee crying for sympathy."

Marc smiled. "I envy you, Eric," he said dryly. "How easy it must be to cut out an appendix! Now take me—"

"Haw!" scoffed Lindstrom. "All you've got to do's ride around on trains."

"Maybe. I've a job for you." Marc unwrapped the meat-smeared wax paper and spread it out on the desk. "There's poison in that meat. Tell me what it is."

Lindstrom's grin widened. "Someone poison one of your conductors, says he hopefully?"

"No. Just a dog."

"A dog? And you come bothering me?"

"I come to the most skilled, most reliable expert in Calumet," replied Marc.

"How to influence people, by Marc Jordan! All right, my boy. I'll analyze it for you. But not right away. To-night."

"That'll do. I'll call you in the morning."

"What's up, Marc? Skullduggery?"

Marc nodded soberly. "A mild term. I'll tell you about it some day. Thanks, Eric."

He heard Lindstrom mutter, "Screwball!" as he closed the door.

The rest of the day provided a terrific workout for Marc's will power. He forced himself to concentrate on distasteful routine until his desk was clear, despite visions of fire and dogs that attempted to intrude. Repeatedly he laid the strips of metal on his desk, glared at them, and resolutely tucked them into his pocket. As a result, by the time he pitched the last letter into the "out" basket he felt whipped. Tired and irritable.

This was his state of mind when he stopped at the brass factory to pick up Nora. She waited on the steps, tripped daintily to the car and slid in beside him.

"Hello, Marc. You're late."

"Had some work to finish."

"Get lots done?"

"No."

"You don't seem very chipper this evening."

"I'm not."

"Gr-rr! The old bear's ouchy!"

"I'm sorry, Nora. My complacency got some jolts to-day."

"Address, Tenth Avenue, I'll bet."

Marc glanced at her quickly. "How'd you guess?"

"Darling! I know you!" Nora slid her hand through the crook of his arm. "When you've got your long nose into something, you're a car on a roller coaster—up and down. You're now down. What's bothering you?"

Marc shuddered involuntarily. "I can't tell you. It's too horrible to think about. And I can't be sure, really sure."

Nora looked steadily at him, real concern clouding her eyes. "Marc, you *are* down."

"Let's forget it," he muttered.

They drove in silence for a while.

"Wonder where Porter was last night?" said Marc, half to himself.

"Why not ask me?"

He stared at her in amazement. "Why? Do you know?"

"Not exactly. But I can guess."

"Go ahead. Guess."

"Well," Nora hesitated, "we had a caller at the office yesterday afternoon. A very nice young man. Fine physique, curly black hair, and the sweetest smile—"

"Never mind the sex appeal," growled Marc. "Come to the point."

"Yes. He delivered a small package to Mr. Porter."

She opened her handbag, carefully checked the arrangement of her hair, and applied a minute dab of powder to her nose.

"Nora," Marc's voice was a file, "I love you! But sometimes I'd like to spank you. What's that got to do with Mr. Porter?"

Nora smiled softly. "A secretary's like the postman; people are so used to them no one ever sees either. Later, when I went into Mr. Porter's office, the box was on his desk. It was blue plush, a jeweler's box. I wonder if Cynthia got a new necklace last night."

Marc's jaw sagged. He gulped.

"I'll bet she didn't," added Nora.

"You vixen, what are you hinting at?"

Nora shot a demure, sidewise glance at him.

"Marc dear, remember how you've criticized me unmercifully for repeating gossip?"

"In this case," replied Marc grimly. "I'll make an exception. I really will. Are you trying to say politely that Porter's doing some two-timing?"

Nora nodded. "That's the gossip." She shook her finger at him. "But you said it. I didn't,"

"But, Nora, that's malicious. How can you know? One box from a jeweler doesn't prove anything."

"Perhaps not. But Mr. Porter's florist bill last month would buy me a lovely fur coat! I don't remember Miriam saying that her mother was deluged with flowers."

"How could I have missed this angle?"

"You don't listen to gossip. Remember?"

11

Anderson pounded his desk with his fist. A soggy cigar stump rolled from one corner of his mouth to the other.

"I'll tell ya straight, Jordan," he growled, "yer nuts. Crazy! I'd be the laughingstock of the town if I listened to you."

Marc sighed wearily. Hands clasped behind his head, feet on Anderson's desk, he stared at the ceiling.

"I'll tell you straight, Jerry," he said slowly, "someone was cremated in Porter's garage last night. I'm convinced of it."

"Rats!"

"Don't you agree these two lumps of leather came from shoe heels?"

"So what? Ever hear of someone leaving a old pair of shoes in a garage?"

"How about the strips of steel?"

Anderson sneered. "You ain't figgered them out yourself. So why should I try?"

Marc banged his feet on the floor and leaned his elbows on the desk. He nodded grudgingly.

"There you're right. But why the neat arrangement of the rack? Why were oil drums stacked along each side with just a nice space for a body between? Tell me that."

Anderson shrugged indifferently. "No, you tell me.

"I am. Jerry, that set-up was deliberate. Why, when the tank blew up, didn't it splatter flaming gas all over the lot? I'll tell you why. Because it was empty! Someone dammed up the front of the storage bin with dirt. When the tank let go it was empty except for fumes. The gasoline was lying in a puddle under the grate.

"I was there. That corner of the garage burned like a blow torch for hours. The fire chief didn't even try to put it out."

Anderson made a futile effort to light his gurgling cigar, gave up, and jammed a fresh one between his lips.

"I agree to this," he said. "The fire looks like arson. But murder? Naw! Did you look around?"

Marc nodded. "I did."

"Did you find anything else? A belt buckle? A watch? A ring? Some change?"

Marc shook his head.

"So. Don't tell me a body can vanish, go up in smoke without leaving a trace."

"It left two shoe heels."

"What do you mean, *it?* Any old shoe heels."

Marc leaned back and hooked his toes around the legs of the chair. He felt beaten. Maybe he was nuts. Maybe Anderson was right. He stared at the inspector for a time. Then he spoke softly.

"Jerry, that storage bin was a most efficient crematory. It had everything: plenty of fuel; a steel rack; good ventilation through the holes in the bottom. And"—he paused a moment—"it had a body! What're you going to do about it?"

"Nothing. Not a darn thing. I'll investigate the possibility of arson, but that's all."

"I think you're wrong, Jerry. Maybe we'll never know. There's mighty little to go on: two pieces of leather and some strips of steel."

"I got my reputation to think of," said Anderson. "Think what the papers'd do to me if I hollered 'Murder' on such flimsy evidence."

"Think what they'll do to you if you don't investigate a murder."

"To have a murder, I gotta have a corpse. You show me a corpse, and I'm with you."

"I am showing you one, practically." Marc pointed to the two black lumps lying on the desk.

"Please, Jordan, let's be sensible about this thing. I'll look into the arson angle. That's all."

"Probably too late for that."

"Why?"

"Porter had a gang of factory laborers out yesterday cleaning the place, hauling the debris away. The evidence, if any, has doubtless been destroyed."

"Um. Why's he in such a helluva hurry to clean up? A mess like that usually stands around for days."

"Why not ask Porter?" said Marc quietly.

"That I'll do."

"Jerry," continued Marc, "you don't subscribe to the cremation theory. Okay. That's your privilege. But if you don't intend to investigate, please keep your mouth shut, will you?"

"Meaning—?"

"Maybe you're right and I'm wrong. But if I am right, I don't want anyone to know I'm suspicious. Don't kid my silly notions in public, particularly where any of the Porter family might pick it up."

"Okay, Jordan, I'll lay off. But, brother, it's a temptation!"

"Thanks, Jerry. Use your phone?"

"Go ahead."

Marc thumbed through the phone book and dialed a number. A girl's voice answered.

"Is Doctor Lindstrom in?" he asked.

"Yes sir. Who's calling, please?"

"Marc Jordan."

A short pause was followed by a man's voice.

"Yes, Marc?"

"Eric, did you have time to analyze the contents of the paper I left you?"

"I did. It was, as you so cleverly deduced, hamburger."

"And what else?"

"Nothing."

Marc's jaw fell slack. "What?"

"Having trouble with your ears? Drop in sometime. I'll give you an examination. I said there's nothing but meat on the paper."

"No poison?"

"Not a trace."

Marc ran his fingers through his hair. "But, Eric, there *must* have been some poison. Are you sure you didn't—" He hesitated. "Are you sure?"

"Believe me, Marc, I know how to make a simple analysis. There was no poison. Have someone else check if you like, but I'll stake my reputation on it."

"I can't believe it!" muttered Marc. "Thanks, Eric."

He stared reproachfully at the telephone.

"Seein' ghosts, Jordan?" asked Anderson curiously.

Marc shook his head. "No. No ghosts where ghosts should be. I can't understand it."

He dialed another number, and again a woman's voice answered.

"Miriam?" he asked.

"Mrs. Porter speaking."

"Oh. Hello, Cynthia. Marc. Your voice is so youthful, I was sure it was your no less beautiful daughter."

Cynthia chuckled. "You're running true to form, Marc."

"I've a silly question to ask. What have you done with Rags?"

"We've disposed of him."

"Buried?"

Cynthia hesitated for a moment, then said slowly, "This's silly too, Marc, but Miriam took Rags' death very hard. She insisted he be given proper canine rites. Doctor Jenkins, the veterinarian, is burying him in his pet graveyard. Rags was one of the family, you know, and it didn't seem right to just dump him out."

"I understand. It's a shame about old Rags. Are you folks staying at home now?"

"Yes. The house is livable, windows fixed and so forth. We, and all our possessions, smell like the inside of a furnace, but that'll wear off."

"You're lucky. The fire could've been lots worse. Thanks, Cynthia."

Hurriedly he riffled through the phone book again, and called yet another number.

"Doctor Jenkins speaking."

"Doctor Jenkins, this's Marc Jordan, chief attorney for the C. and M. Railroad. I'm a good friend of the Porter family."

"Oh yes, Mr. Jordan. I've heard of you."

"Understand you're disposing of the carcass of the Porters' pet dog, Rags?"

"That's correct. We'll bury him today."

"I've reason to suspect, Doctor, that Rags was poisoned. It's a shame to destroy a valuable animal. If my guess is right, the guilty one should be caught and punished. I presume you're equipped to make chemical analyses?"

"Yes, I could make simple tests for poison."

"Will you, please?"

"Why, I guess so. I don't see anything wrong in it."

"I'd be very glad if you would. I'll pay the expenses."

"I'll take care of it."

"Another thing. The Porters have had several shocks lately. I'd rather not upset them. Whatever the results, please say nothing to them about it."

"Surely, Mr. Jordan."

Anderson chuckled as Marc hung up for the third time.

"You oily son-of-a-gun!" he said. "Sneakin' around behind, smellin' dead dogs."

"I'm allergic to dead dogs," snapped Marc. "They shouldn't die by violence. It's happened before. 'Bye, Jerry."

Marc rapidly strode from the building, dodged through pedestrian traffic for several blocks and entered another office. He was pensive as he rode up in the elevator, and was still thoughtful when he entered Thatcher's anteroom. Thatcher's bodyguard and doorkeeper, the bald-headed ape with enormous arms, was busy cleansing his fingernails. He gave Marc a blank, suspicious stare.

"Thatcher in?"

"Yeah."

"May I see him?"

The man finished a thumb nail, jabbed the knife into the top of his desk, and leaned through the inner door. In a few seconds he swung the door open, jerked his thumb toward the interior, and returned to his manicuring.

Marc strode into the inner sanctum. Thatcher sat as usual with his palms flat on his empty desk. His face wore a questioning frown.

"Sit down, Jordan. What's on your mind?"

Marc dropped into a chair against the wall and proceeded to load his pipe before answering.

"Complaints, Thatcher, and your latest report."

"What complaints?"

"Klutz hasn't been doing so well the last few nights. He tells me he lost Meegan in the Tenth Avenue neighborhood night before last."

"Klutz," replied Thatcher flatly, "has been doing as well as any man could. He's the best man I have, and that says he's good."

"Fact remains he lost Meegan on at least two occasions. By coincidence, on each occasion activity flared up in the Porter case. I don't like coincidences that come in bunches. They begin to lose their coincidental appearance."

"That," said Thatcher dryly, "is a mouthful of two-bit words, meaning—?"

Marc sucked steadily on his pipe.

"I persuaded Mr. Porter to engage you to protect his life and property, and the lives and property of his family. You haven't delivered."

Thatcher's face went white and his bushy eyebrows drew together. His voice continued in the same flat tone. The palms of his hands drew little circles on the desk.

"Let me explain something to you, Jordan. In my business, we don't guarantee results. We do our best. That's been done. If you don't like it, get the blazes out of here. Take your lousy job somewhere else. See if you can get better service."

Marc balanced his chair on its back legs and returned Thatcher's glare.

"All right, Thatcher. I know you're the best outfit in town. I wouldn't have come to you if you weren't. However, I think it a serious matter that Meegan gave you the slip. I don't suppose Klutz is around?"

Without comment, Thatcher pressed a button under his desk and returned his hands to the desk top. In a moment Klutz entered, a battered hat cocked at a belligerent angle and a cigarette drooping from the corner of his mouth.

"Call me, Boss?" he asked, darting a defiant glance at Marc.

Thatcher jerked his head in Marc's direction.

"Mike," said Marc, unable to suppress his curiosity, "when do you sleep?"

Klutz grinned sourly. "I don't! Ain't had a good sleep, in bed, for years."

"Jordan's sore," said Thatcher, "because you lost Meegan again."

"Gees," bristled Klutz, "whadda ya expect? That guy's like a eel."

"Not sore, Mike; just disappointed. I'm fighting a nasty situation, alone and without official support. If you can keep track of Meegan, that'd at least eliminate one suspicious gentleman."

"I done my best," said Klutz.

"Where's Meegan now?"

"Dunno. We ain't been able to pick him up. He ain't been home, and he ain't been to none of his hangouts."

"You mean you haven't seen him since the fire?"

"That's right."

Marc frowned thoughtfully for a moment.

"D'you suppose he skipped town?"

Klutz shrugged. "Could be. But he ain't picked up the junk from his room. I made what ya might call judicious inquiries."

"Do you want us to continue work on the case, Jordan?" asked Thatcher.

"Of course!" barked Marc. "Now more than ever. Heaven knows what'll happen next." He leaped to his feet and paced about the office. "This case stinks!"

"How?" said Thatcher. "You've never told us what you're worried about."

Marc shook his head. "I trust your discretion, Thatcher. But there's too much at stake to bandy words." He turned to Klutz. "Did you ever see Meegan go into a meat market?"

"Huh?" said Klutz. "Gosh no. Bars and dives, but no meat market."

Marc tore a sheet from his notebook and scribbled a hurried note which he handed to Klutz.

"Take this to Doctor Lindstrom. He'll give you a piece of wax paper such as is used to wrap meat, ground meat. Canvass stores handling meat. I'm interested in those open late at night. Hunt for stores using that paper and then see if you can get the description of anyone buying a package about ten-thirty night before last."

Puzzled, Klutz glanced at the note and then at Thatcher.

"Okay," said Thatcher. "Go ahead."

"Just a minute," said Marc. "Where does Meegan live?"

"Southeast Avenue," said Klutz. "It's a punk roomin' house down near the power station."

Marc nodded. "I know where it is. Who's Meegan been seeing much of?"

"Nobody, 'cept that beat up bag, Trixie Donovan. Buys her drinks at the Purple Pot about every night."

"Let me know what you find out about that paper."

"Yeah," said Klutz, disappearing through the door. Marc started to follow, then hesitated.

"By the way," he said, turning back to Thatcher, "what's Joel Porter been up to?"

"Nothing. That is, nothing unusual. A lot of tearing around and wild parties, but we've had no trouble keeping track of him."

"That was a bad lead," muttered Marc. "Thanks, Thatcher."

Marc was about to press the elevator button when he glanced at his watch. It was almost noon and he decided to drop in on his friend Oscar Witherspoon, attorney at law, whose offices were in the same building. He trotted down a flight of steps and entered Witherspoon's office.

The occupant glanced up with surprised pleasure. Witherspoon was taller than Marc and twenty pounds lighter.

A gray fuzz circled the bald area on the top of his head. Good-natured crows had left footprints at the corners of his eyes and his lips habitually tilted up, a fact which misled many an opponent at the bar.

"You've made enough money this morning, Oscar," said Marc. "Come on. I'll buy you a lunch."

"You bet you will," chuckled Witherspoon. "You still owe me one for that last game of chess!"

"You were lucky. I had you mated in three moves, except—"

"Ya! Ya! Except! Many a man's been a millionaire—except!"

Witherspoon rose and limped to a hat rack. One leg was slightly shorter than the other, due to an accident. He laid his hand on Marc's shoulder affectionately as they left the office together.

Finding a table in a remote corner of a quiet restaurant across the street, they ordered lunch. Witherspoon inserted a cigarette in a silver holder and offered the case to Marc.

"No thanks," he said. "I'll stick to my hod."

"This is a pleasure, Marc. Haven't seen much of you lately. What're you up to?"

"Busy. But not, I must admit, exclusively with company business."

Witherspoon's eyes twinkled. "I knew it. I can tell by the gleam in your eye and the sag of your shoulders. Why won't you come in as my partner? I've asked you often enough."

"Run of the mill legal work—I want none of it. Much prefer railroading. Of course, once in a while an outstanding problem comes up that makes me wonder."

"Make you some real money, Marc."

"I'll think it over. Right now, Oscar, I'm worried, very worried. There's no one I can talk to but you, and I must talk to someone."

"Of course you're worried. Can't fool me. Go ahead. Shoot."

Marc hesitated. "You won't laugh?"

"Marc, my boy, I got past the laughing stage thirty-five years ago. Now, out with it."

"I'll start at the beginning. About six weeks ago, Dolly Porter was killed in a crossing accident on the eve of her wedding. You remember that?"

"Yes, of course."

"You may remember that her rejected suitor, Ted Arthur, died at the same time. I thought at first, and most people still think, that Dolly was favoring Ted with a good-bye ride, and the car was accidentally struck. But that didn't look right."

Witherspoon chuckled. "Things never look right to you, Marc."

Marc bristled. "Laugh, darn you. But they didn't. There were many things. The engineer said the car was standing at the crossing, yet a car won't stand without a brake, because of the grade. My second opinion, which Anderson now subscribes to, was that Ted deliberately parked on the crossing and killed them both. But that won't wash.

"Ted's body was outside the car. Blood was smeared on the outside of the door. Bits of his clothing were snagged in the jagged metal, also outside. Furthermore, the fireman saw the lights of a second car, parked behind Dolly's at the instant of the crash. Tread marks identified this car as Ted's. It was gone when the crew got back to the wreck, and we found it parked beside Porter's house.

"Here's what I think really happened. Someone drove Dolly's car to the crossing with Dolly in it, either dead or unconscious, intending that it should appear an accident. Ted, having just left his date, saw Dolly's car and followed. When he found her car parked at the crossing, he frantically tried to get her out, and died in the attempt.

Then the murderer seized opportunity by the horns and
escaped by driving Ted's car back to Porter's, leaving it
there to account for their being together."

"Marc, you're a mole!"

"It's not funny, Oscar, as I've tried to tell you."

"I know it. I marvel at, and admire, your stubbornness.
What are you doing about it?"

"The story's not finished. Nothing happened for two or
three weeks. Then one night, with no warning whatsoever,
Miriam, Dolly's sister, was shot at."

"Shot at?"

"Yes. From the street. The police picked up a hoodlum,
one Slats Meegan, in the neighborhood, but had to turn
him loose. That closed that episode. Then a week later,
Miriam was kidnaped. Surely you read about it in the papers?"

"Yes, but she turned up the next day, drunk. All the
earmarks of a big party."

"Maybe." Marc hesitated and scowled at his plate. "It
does look a little fishy. She was doped, but otherwise unharmed. Again nothing came of it. Which brings us up to
night before last."

Witherspoon watched Marc in silence and then waved
to a waitress.

"We're going to need a drink!" he said dryly. "Two
old-fashioneds."

"Night before last, two significant things occurred:
Rags, the Porters' faithful old watch dog, died; and their
garage burned down."

Marc sipped his drink and stirred the remainder ab-
sently.

"Arson?" asked Witherspoon.

"Unquestionably. Now, Oscar, here's where you have
my permission to laugh. Call me a sadist, if you wish. Porter, like the darn fool he is, had several hundred gallons of

gasoline stored in his garage. That gasoline burned in one corner for several hours. Burned like a plumber's furnace. The firemen just let it go.

"Next morning, yesterday, I looked at that corner. It was a crematory!"

"What!" Witherspoon choked on his drink, spilled it on the table and coughed violently into his napkin. Regaining the use of his breathing apparatus, he squinted at Marc.

"That got you, huh?" said Marc. "It got me too. Someone built a mud dam under a metal rack in the corner, and drained the gasoline into a puddle under it. On the rack was laid a body!"

"But, Marc," gasped Witherspoon, "that's hideous. What are you and Anderson waiting for?"

Marc smiled grimly. "No corpse! The cremating was well done. So well that nothing was left. What little body ash or debris there may have been was washed away by the fire hoses."

"You mean to say that this is pure conjecture?"

"Not entirely. There were two items: several metal strips neatly arranged and practically welded to the frame; two bits of leather, shoe heels which apparently dropped through the grate and weren't completely consumed."

"And the police?"

"Are laughing. Great, deep belly laughs. Anderson says I'm nuts. Maybe." Distracted, Marc ran his fingers through his hair. "It was a shock to me, my wits refused to work. Before I thought to stop them, Porter's men had the mess cleaned up. If I'd only had sense to photograph that set-up. It was cleverly done."

"Marc," said Witherspoon soberly, "no wonder you're worried. Can I help?"

"I hope so. I know it sounds like a delirium dream, discussing it this way. But fiendish things are happening at the Porters'."

"Who do you think was burned?"

A shudder shook Marc's lanky body. "I haven't the slightest idea. That's what makes it so outlandish and difficult."

"Do you have any reason to suspect any member of the family?"

"Yes and no. For instance, I just learned that Don has been doing some philandering."

"My boy, where've you been? That's not news."

"It was to me. Then Joel's a wild son-of-a-gun. He's gotten into serious trouble several times. But I can't tie him in. Cynthia's high-strung and intense, and Aunt Sarah's a God-fearin' old biddy who, if she thought she read God's will aright, might do anything." Marc paused to finish his drink. "Miriam was in love with Karl Snyder. She *might* have faked the shot and the kidnaping. Trouble is, at each crisis all the members of the family were unaccounted for.

"Always lurking in the shadows is this Slats Meegan character, and still further back his run down girl friend."

"You haven't said yet how I can help."

"I want some family history. The Porter family. You've known them for many years. Go 'way back."

Witherspoon smoked quietly and he studied Marc meditatively.

"Way back, eh? You knew, I presume, that Don and Cynthia were married before?"

Marc nodded.

"Porter's life, at least the part exposed to public view, was lacking in sparkle. He went to work for his father, finally took over the business. He married a local girl—can't recall her name. Dolly was born of that marriage. Dolly must've been two or three when her mother died.

"Cynthia was different. She had color. I remember her well. The spark plug of her class, she starred in dramatics, school plays. Her name was often in the paper as queen of the wheat festival, chairman of the Junior Prom and so forth. You know the type of vivacious youngster.

"She went to the University a couple of years. Studied dramatics. The second summer, much against her parent's wishes, she toured with a summer stock company playing the whistle stops. At the end of the summer, she ran away and turned up in Hollywood.

"For several years she dropped out of the public eye. Her father was a Mason and a good friend of mine. He liked to play chess, too. The day he died, a letter arrived from Cynthia saying she was married and had a baby daughter. Mrs. James was numb with shock at her husband's death, and this news increased it. Anyway, Cynthia didn't come home.

"One day, a couple of years later, Cynthia appeared with Miriam. Her husband had been killed in an auto accident, and she was coming home to Mother. She studied stenography, went to work as Porter's secretary, married him a few years later. There you have it.

"Joel's their son." Witherspoon paused, then continued slowly, "Joel I don't understand. A wild one, he seems to combine the bad characteristics of both parents. He is so different from either of the girls."

"Something I've wondered," said Marc, "did Porter adopt Miriam? I never felt like asking."

Witherspoon shook his head. "No. He tried. I worked up papers for him once. But Cynthia, for some reason, flatly refused. However, Miriam is known by, and has always used, the name 'Porter.'"

"Adoption proceedings would simplify her inheritance, in case of Porter's death."

"Of course. I made the point, but to no avail."

"Oscar, you're a director of the bank, aren't you?"

"That's right."

"As an officer, couldn't you peek at the Porter family bank accounts?"

Witherspoon's eyes twinkled. "Maybe. But I couldn't divulge any information. Not if I want to stay free, white, and sixty-six!"

"I know," replied Marc dryly, "but you could drop a little hint, couldn't you? In confidence?"

"What are you driving at?"

"I recall a bit of dinner table conversation at the Porters' the night of Dolly's death. Dolly said Miriam was broke, in spite of the fact that Don has been giving each of the girls a birthday check of a thousand dollars for years. I'm curious about it. Also, I'm curious about Porter's expenses—florist, jeweler, and so forth."

"You're toying with dynamite, Marc."

Marc beat the table with his fist.

"Oscar," he snapped, "two and probably three people have died! Other numbers may be up. How do we know? What's a little snooping compared to that?"

"Good point," replied Witherspoon. "All right. I've stuck my neck out before, legally speaking. I'll see what I can find."

"Thanks, Oscar. I thought you would."

12

A mat of hair covered Thatcher's wrists and thinned out
along the backs of his fingers. His thick hands, folded
over the slight protuberance of his stomach, looked like
the claws of a gorilla. A shaded floor lamp beside the out-
size leather rocker in which he sat cast shadows across his
face and made his eyebrows appear as streaks of coal. He
rocked slowly and rhythmically.

Opposite slouched Klutz. He half lay, half sat in a corner of the davenport, thumbs hooked in his vest. He had
dispensed with the protection of a hat, an unaccustomed
formality. His face was twisted sideways, one eye half
closed, to avoid the curling smoke of a cigarette.

The sumptuously furnished room was thick with silence. Thatcher peered at an assortment of objects lying
in the crumpled folds of a newspaper. With thumb and
forefinger, he picked up an expensive watch from which
dangled a heavy gold chain with a pocket knife attached.
He poked at a miscellany of other items: an automatic
pencil; a dollar or two in change; a man's belt.

He grunted, and scowled at Klutz.

"What do you think about this?" he asked, indicating
the contents of the newspaper.

"Ain't paid to think, Boss," replied Klutz, exhaling a cloud
of smoke through his nostrils. "Just leg work, that's me."

141

A sour smile tugged at the corners of Thatcher's mouth.

"You," he said, "are a cynic."

"Cynic? That what I am?"

Thatcher examined the watch more closely. He pressed the stem and snapped open the cover.

"I wonder if this junk would interest Jordan?"

Klutz shrugged. "Could be." He stamped out his cigarette in a silver tray and cast a yearning look at the sideboard.

"Go ahead, Mike," said Thatcher, reaching for the telephone on a low stand beside his chair.

Klutz poured a tumbler half full of liquor, added a dash of soda water, and slumped again into the davenport. Thatcher fumbled with the phone dial.

"Jordan speaking."

"Thatcher. Got time to stop in at my apartment?"

"Something important?"

"I think so. Klutz has information about your hamburger customer, and we've something else to show you."

"I'll be right over."

Thatcher returned the telephone to its cradle and sank back in his chair. No word was spoken during the fifteen minutes that followed. Klutz, savoring the contents of his glass, was well begun on a second when Marc, tense of face, entered with quick strides.

He studied Thatcher's lounging, bathrobe-swathed hulk, and shot an inquiring glance at Klutz.

Thatcher waved him to a chair.

"Sit down," he said. "Drink?"

Marc shook his head, still watching Klutz.

"What did you learn about the wax paper, Mike?" he asked.

Klutz very carefully, very cautiously, set his glass on the floor and deliberately lit a cigarette.

"Well," he said, "I find a store uses the paper, and sells hamburger."

"I was sure you would," said Marc impatiently. "What else?"

"Don't rush me," replied Klutz. "There's a couple of 'em. A one-man cockroach nest up the street a ways from the Porters' looks hot."

"Yes?"

"Seems a sawed off gent come a coupla nights ago and bought a pound o' hamburger. The butcher remembers him on account of he was missin' the bottom of one ear. That's him! Old Slatsy in the flesh, the dirty tramp!"

Marc felt the perspiration stand out on his face. He sank into a chair, pushed his hat off his forehead, and swabbed his cheeks with his handkerchief.

"Did you see Meegan go in there?"

"No. I told you that."

"Then it was after he got away from you."

"Yeah. That ape ducks me, then goes and buys hamburger. What fer? A picnic?"

Marc smiled grimly. "It was a picnic, all right."

"What *did* he buy it for, Jordan?" Thatcher asked.

"To feed to Porter's dog."

Thatcher allowed himself a faint chuckle. "I see why you're interested."

"That's good, Mike," said Marc. "You mentioned something else."

Thatcher tilted his head toward the end table. "This junk."

Marc rose, walked over to Thatcher and stood gazing curiously at the odds and ends in the newspaper.

"You tell him, Mike."

"I'm settin' in the park tonight, watchin' the Porters' like I got orders to do. Somebody throwed something into the bushes along the edge. I didn't think nothin' of it right off. Then, havin' nothin' else to do, I goes nosin' around and finds this bundle."

Marc's mild curiosity slowly changed to surprise and a thrill of excitement. He arrested an impulse to pick up the watch, and wheeled on Klutz like a tiger.

"You're saying this package was discarded across from the Porters'. By whom?"

Klutz shook his head. "Ya got me. All I seen was a dame in the next block. Mebbe she throwed it, mebbe not."

"Did anyone come out of the Porters'?"

"Mebbe. I didn't see no one."

"I hope you haven't touched these things," said Marc, rolling the paper around the articles.

"I picked up the watch," said Thatcher, "by the edge. Nothing else has been touched."

Marc tucked the package into his pocket. "Good. I'll take that drink now."

"Fix him up, Mike," said Thatcher. "Have one myself."

Marc again sank into his chair, threw one leg over the arm and allowed his head to fall against the cushions. He sat thus while Klutz fussed with glasses.

"Mike," said Marc, half emptying his glass, "instead of doing guard duty in the park the rest of the night, you're coming with me."

"Where?"

"Reconnaissance. Attack the enemy in the rear."

"Where's this rear located?" asked Thatcher suspiciously.

Marc twirled his glass, held it up to the light to admire the color. "I'm going to examine the domicile of one Slats Meegan, by fair means or foul."

"Um-mm. Who takes the rap, if the means are foul?"

"I do."

"You bet. I won't, nor will Klutz. We stay out of trouble."

"Of that," said Marc ironically, "I'm well aware."

Thatcher made a tent of his hairy fingers. "Rubbing it in, aren't you, Jordan?"

"What do you mean?"

"Porter's paying the bill; you're having all the fun."

Marc shot a quick, sidewise glance at him.

"In his interest," he said calmly.

"Sure—sure."

"How you figger to get in this domicile?" interposed Klutz.

"We'll work that out when we get there, Mike. Let's go."

Marc drained his glass while Klutz reluctantly transferred his hat from the floor to his head. Silently, Thatcher's eyes followed them out.

"What's Meegan's layout?" asked Marc, as they drove through deserted streets.

"Just a punk roomin' house. He's gotta room."

"A family affair?"

"Naw. Dame named Snead runs it. Her customers're mostly linemen from the power company."

"Do you know her?"

"Talked to her, if that's knowin' her."

"Is she likely to be amenable to reason?"

"Huh?"

"Would she let us into Meegan's room?"

"Doubt it. You could try, though. Turn right here. Now, the fourth house on the left."

Marc stopped in the shadows at the curb with the motor idling.

"One would need to count, at that," he said. "All the houses in the block were built during the same nightmare!"

"Two blocks. The next street don't cut through."

Marc studied the unprepossessing dwelling, a three-story affair. One pale light gleamed from a third-floor window. A narrow walk separated each house from its neighbor. The street was deserted and dark, illuminated only by the feeble glint of an inadequate light on the corner.

"Which is Meegan's room?"

"Second floor rear. Over the kitchen."

"You're sure?"

"Yeah. Seen him there. You goin' in by the front door?"

Marc was silent for a moment.

"I don't think so," he said finally. "At this time of night, and considering Mrs. Snead's probable character, chances are I wouldn't get in. And get in I will. If Mrs. S. spots me asking about Meegan, and then his room's raided, I'm a roast duck. No. The indirect approach is best."

Marc drove the length of the block and turned left. At the entrance to the alley, he dimmed his lights and very slowly drifted along behind the houses. The alley was paved, lined with garages and a miscellany of outbuildings. He peered through squinted eyes at the dim outline of the Snead mansion.

Continuing to the street, he turned and entered the alley again, heading in the opposite direction. Pulling onto the apron of a garage behind Snead's, he shut off the lights and throttled the motor, then sat a while, thinking.

Tossing his hat onto the back seat, he sidled out to the car, shucked off his topcoat and tossed it after the hat. Klutz fidgeted.

"Looky, Jordan," he whispered hoarsely, "I ain't catchin' no house-breakin' rap."

"Relax!" snapped Marc softly. "Pile out. Let the engine idle, and have the doors ajar."

Protesting with a string of muttered oaths, Klutz complied.

"Cop comes by, I don't know you! Never seen you before."

"All right. If I get in trouble, you run and hide, if you must. In the meantime, I'm going over the back porch roof into Meegan's room."

Marc picked up a handful of pebbles and pressed them into Klutz's hand.

"Here. Stand by the end of the garage. If anyone comes, throw a pebble or two against the window."

"You damn fool!" growled Klutz. "We could get a couple years for this!"

"Think of the time you'd have for rest. Keep your eyes and ears open."

Marc crept silently through the opening between two low buildings, treading as though on eggs, followed by Klutz. On reaching the end, he paused and studied the dark, shadowy building before him. The silence was oppressive. The tiny sound of their feet on the brick wall crashed like gunfire.

Touching Klutz on the arm, Marc crept forward, placing each foot cautiously to avoid a chance garbage can or milk bottle. He arrived at the porch without mishap and stepped up. He felt along the corner post supporting the roof and located a clothesline hook. Mounting to the rail, he could easily reach the gutter. With one foot on the hook, he strained with arms and shoulders, threw the other leg over the edge and rolled his body onto the roof. He crouched for a moment, listening.

The flat tin roof cracked and buckled agonizingly as he slid his body to the window. After several moments of tugging and prying, he managed to slide the sash open. Then he stepped into the room and stood rigid, holding his breath, and straining to catch any sound. The silence was that of a tomb.

The window-shade he pulled down tightly, stepped carefully to a second window on the other wall and did likewise. He slipped a pen-size flashlight from his vest pocket and, shading the glow with his hand, threw the tiny point of light about the room.

It was small and bare. No curtains graced the windows, and a thin reed rug was the only floor covering. Along the far wall stood a narrow iron bed with a dressing table containing several drawers at the end. A small table was placed under the side window and held a portable radio. A badly worn, very dirty chair completed the furnishings.

There were two doors, one in each wall opposite the windows. Marc tiptoed across the room and tried the first. It was locked. He played his light along the jamb and found a night latch securing it. The second door gave into a closet with an assortment of clothes, a raincoat, a suit, on hangers. On the floor stood a battered traveling case.

Marc turned from the closet and pulled out the first of the dresser drawers. It contained a collection of gentlemen's apparel—shirts, underwear, and a bundle of more or less clean socks.

The second drawer was empty. The third held a jumbled wad of dirty clothes. He pawed through them, finding nothing except one item which he passed over, and then picked up. It was odd. He spread it out on the dresser top curiously.

The garment was of peculiar shape, much like a bloated hour glass. Marc's pulse quickened as he examined it. Along one side was a harness arrangement of straps. Two or more thicknesses of cloth had been used, sewed together by closely spaced, parallel stitching, the space between forming narrow pockets.

Marc emitted a long low gasp. Excitement beating at his temples, he fumbled with the edge of the garment, and from one of the pockets drew a thin, narrow, tough yet pliable strip of metal. He flexed it between his fingers, then tucked it into his pocket.

His spine tingled at a soft click at the door. He froze, and waited. The click was repeated, then a rattle as though someone were trying to enter. For the space of a score of tremulous breaths, there was no further sound. Marc placed his ear against the door panel. The other intruder had apparently left.

Driven by a sense of danger, yet wishing to miss nothing, Marc turned to the closet. He felt rapidly through pockets and along the shelf. Then he focused his light on the traveling case. After some fumbling, it snapped open to disclose a metal box: a small version of the type used for fishing tackle. Otherwise the case was empty.

Using his handkerchief to shield his hand, Marc set the box on the dresser. With his thumbnail, he cautiously released the spring catch and lifted the lid. A collection of papers met his eye. Raising these, he gulped. Filling the lower half of the box lay a pile of money—several thousand dollars. Beside the money was a smaller tin box. This, when he pried it open, proved to contain a handful of pistol shells.

Marc picked up the money, hesitated a moment, then stuffed it into a pocket of the traveling case. The box he wrapped in a towel. He was just completing the wrapping when there was a sharp click at the window glass, followed by another, and another. He bounded to the window, cautiously raised the shade, and peered into the night.

Faint, muffled by distance, the frightening wail of a police siren jarred against his ears. It grew louder by the second. He hopped over the sill and slid to the edge of the roof. Laying the package in the gutter, he swung his body over the side, where he dangled from one hand while the other pawed for the box. Then, with it pressed to his stomach, he dropped to the ground. At that instant the police car, with a banshee shriek, skidded to a stop at the front of the house.

Marc sprinted to the car just as Klutz, frantic and trembling, stood about to take off on foot.

"Get in!" growled Marc. "Quick!"

He slid the car into gear and started with a jerk. As they got under way, a beam of light flicked through from the street, followed by a hoarse shout:

"There he goes!"

The police car started with a roar. Between the houses, they could see and hear it speeding along on a parallel course.

"Trapped, you fool!" snarled Klutz. "Pinched!"

Marc jammed the accelerator to the floor, and the gray Ford bounded forward like a streak of black night.

"Shut up!" he barked, peering with desperate concentration into the inky gloom of the alley. As he neared the intersection, he slowed slightly and suddenly tramped on the brake, bringing the car to an abrupt halt. With a skillful, reckless, wheeling sweep, he backed into the yawning cavern of an empty garage.

"Spotted this before," he muttered. "Close your door! Fast!"

Klutz, no fool and quick to catch an idea, slid out one side of the car and Marc out the other. Each seized a door and swung it shut. The center latch clicked a second before the police car, tires screaming in protest, spun into the alley and snarled past.

Instantly, Marc eased his door open and Klutz did likewise. He peeked at the angry taillights of the receding car, then sprang back to the wheel.

"Watch 'em, Mike!" he said in a soft, brittle voice. "See which way they turn."

Tensely, Klutz peered around the door jamb.

"At the corner," he said hoarsely, "they stopped, moving slow, turned right!" He bounded into his seat.

"Here we go," breathed Marc, skidding into the alley and continuing in the direction they had been going originally. At the street he too turned right, then left at the corner, making the turn on no more than two wheels. Klutz, breathing in nervous gasps, squirmed around and watched through the rear window. Marc ducked right and left, zigzagging for a dozen blacks, gradually reducing speed until they were traveling at a leisurely thirty miles per hour.

Little by little, Marc relaxed. Klutz, huddled limply beside him, mopped his face and nervously lit a cigarette.

"Gee!" he gasped. "That was too damn close!"

Marc nodded silently. He drove for another five minutes, and turned into Eastwood Avenue. Klutz stiffened.

"Hey! Yer goin' the wrong way!"

Marc smiled grimly. "Understand there's been a robbery at Snead's. We really should go and see the fun!"

"Yer crazy! What if the cops spots ya?"

"No one saw us—enough," said Marc easily. "I'd like to see what goes on."

"Okay, brother. You just picked me up. Remember? Saw me standin' on a corner."

Marc chuckled. "That's right, Mike. I just picked you up."

They approached Mrs. Snead's residence at a moderate, strictly legal pace. The police car was parked at the curb, and the house was a glare of light. A knot of people stood talking on the doorstep, and the flicker of a flashlight could be seen in the rear.

"Hope you didn't drop yer wallet," said Klutz.

"So do I," agreed Marc fervently.

He cut across town and paused beside the Tenth Avenue park.

"Here you are, Mike," he said, "back on your beat."

"Praise the Lord," replied Klutz. "Be glad to see the last o' you!"

In his apartment, a few minutes later, Marc was relieved to find that Tony was still out. He set the package on his desk, untied the towel wrapping, and pried open the box.

The top paper was a folded poster. He opened it curiously. A front and side view of a thick-jowled, stubble-bearded man stared back at him. Plainly visible was the mutilated lobe of his left ear.

*Wanted! For Murder!—Slats Meegan, alias Tony
Alberts, alias Jackson—*

More details followed.

Marc whistled. Even hoodlums keep scrap books! He
riffled through the rest of the papers and, laying them
aside, turned his attention to the box of shells. He dumped
the contents onto his blotter. There were several dozen
bullets, and one spent slug of the same calibre as the
others. This Marc rolled around with his finger. The others
he scraped back into the box.

He reached into a drawer and extricated a small pill
box on which was scribbled a date, and one word: "Miriam." Opening the lid, he dropped the contents, a slug of
similar size and shape, onto the blotter beside the first.
Burying his chin in his hands, he stared at the two ugly
bits of metal.

13

Whistling softly under his breath, Marc mounted the steps of the Municipal Building two at a time. Nearing the top, he stopped, turned and made his way to a drug store. He walked directly to a phone booth and ruffled through the directory, laying the package he was carrying on the desk beside him.

Entering the booth, he dropped a coin. His hand was halfway to the dial when he hesitated, let the receiver dangle, darted back to the desk and retrieved the bundle. Then he completed the call. A brisk voice answered.

"Good morning. Doctor Jenkins."

"Jordan, Doctor. I asked you to test the Porters' dog, Rags, for possible poison."

"Yes, Mr. Jordan. I've made the test. The stomach contents showed a considerable concentration of poison. Arsenic. Sufficient for death, I'd say."

"I thought so!" Marc paused. "Don't suppose you could tell the medium used to administer the dose?"

"No. That's beyond me. I can give you a specimen. Possibly you could get it done elsewhere."

"It may be necessary. Maybe not. What do I owe you?"

"Nothing. The test is quite simple, and there'll be no charge."

"Thanks, Doctor."

Marc felt elated, and yet confused, as he retraced his steps to the police building. He nodded to the desk officer and ran up the stairs to Anderson's hole in the wall.

The inspector appeared cocky and confident. A freshly lighted cigar tilted from the corner of his mouth at a rakish angle, and his eyes, magnified by the thick lenses, almost twinkled.

"The nutty guys you see, barging in and out of this dump," he growled.

"Morning, Jerry." Marc sank into a chair, propped his feet on the desk, and dropped his hat over the horn of a dictaphone. "Why the unbecoming cheerfulness? You seem happy."

Anderson chuckled and flipped cigar ash on the floor.

"Sure," he said. "Gotta have good days once in a while. We just hung the Penny Company robbery on the right guy."

"Unusual," said Marc.

"What's on what you use for brains?" Anderson stared at him suspiciously. "You never make me no social calls."

Marc loaded his pipe before replying. The carefully wrapped package he held in his lap.

"You're a mind reader, Jerry. A short time ago, we had a discussion about a gentleman named Meegan."

"Here we go!" snorted Anderson.

"You were going to look him up. Have you?"

"Yeah." Anderson struggled to his feet and waddled over to a file case. Ruffling through a drawer full of folders, he selected one and returned. He unwound the string catch and dumped a sheaf of papers on the desk.

"Goon from Chi," he continued. "Livin' here in Calumet on that new leaf he turned over. Five feet six, a hundred and eighty pounds, brown hair, blue eyes, lobe of his left ear gone. Here's his map." Anderson slid a police picture across the desk.

Marc glanced at it perfunctorily. He'd seen it before.

"That what you want?"

"Not exactly," said Marc slowly. "What's he been doing the last twenty years?"

"Time, mostly." Anderson thumbed through more papers. "First stretch was in Los Angeles just about twenty years back. Robbery. He showed up in Chicago and was tried for murder. Acquitted. Lack of evidence. Then he did two or three short stretches. He got out about a year ago on three years of a five-year stretch. We checked him, but he's a good boy now."

"Is that a fact!" mused Marc. "The murder acquittal—what's the story?"

"Some squirrel was shot in bed. Through the neck. A beat cop recognized Meegan and remembered seein' him in the neighborhood, so they put out a call and picked him up. But they couldn't hang him. There wasn't even a bullet for evidence. The slug went clean through the guy's neck and the murderer was cute enough to dig it outa the bed and take it along."

"Cute indeed! I see he has lots of aliases. What's his right name?"

"Meegan." Anderson's round cheeks bounced with laughter. "Here's a good one—for a crook. He's called 'Slats'; know why?"

"Maybe," replied Marc, smiling inwardly, "but I'd like to hear your version."

"He's gotta weak back. Wears a corset! Imagine, a hood wearin' a corset!"

"Ridiculous. And yet even a crook should be allowed the pleasure of a weak back. How do you know he's been good?"

"Ain't had no complaints."

"I made one," said Marc softly.

"Oh, well, you, Jordan!" Anderson replied derisively. "Hell's bells!"

"You may live to regret that," replied Marc. Carefully, he started to unwrap the package in his lap. "Meyers around?"

"Meyers? Think so. Why?"

"If he's not busy, may I borrow him?"

"Borrow him, to go out somewhere?"

"No. I brought the sample."

Anderson shrugged condescendingly. He glanced at Marc's package, then barked into the telephone.

"Meyers there? Send him in." He turned to Marc. "Whatcha got?"

"A secret."

A slight, wizened, middle-aged man with a cynical twist to his mouth entered softly and stood before Anderson.

"Send for me, Boss?"

Anderson nodded toward Marc, who carefully slid the box, nestled in its wrappings, onto the desk.

"You'll probably find my fingerprints on that box, Meyers. Tell me who else touched it."

Meyers picked up the box, also holding it gingerly with the paper, and started for the door. Marc stopped him.

"Here," he said, "take this with you. Keep it handy to look at." He handed him Meegan's fingerprint card.

There followed a few minutes of desultory chatter before Meyers returned. He stepped softly through the door and placed the box on the desk.

"Meegan," he said flatly.

"Huh?" Anderson's cigar twitched violently and sprayed ash down his shirt front. "Meegan's prints are on that box?"

"Right, Boss."

Anderson spun his chair around and glowered suspiciously at Marc.

"Where'd you get the box, Jordan?"

"Picked it up." Marc polished the bowl of his pipe against the side of his nose. "Interesting box. Now, try this." He drew a smaller package from his coat pocket, unwrapped it, and laid it beside the box.

Anderson stared at the watch, chain and knife lying beside a shiny pencil in the folds of the paper.

"Now what?" he demanded. "Where'd you get this junk?"

"It, too, was picked up," replied Marc evasively. "Dust it, Meyers. See what you find."

Again Meyers disappeared with the bundle. He was gone much longer. Anderson, ignoring Marc, waded into routine business.

Nervous and impatient, Marc prowled about the office. He turned expectantly at the click of the door.

"What did you find?" he asked eagerly.

Meyers placidly placed the paper on the desk and stared at Marc.

"Nothing," he said.

"Nothing?" Disappointment struck him like a blow in the face. His voice was incredulous. "You mean there are no fingerprints?"

"Yup. That's what I mean. Some smudges along the edge, but nothin' I can read."

"Did you check the knife blade?"

"Yup."

Marc picked up the watch and sank into a chair. He glared at it silently, pressed the stem and popped open the cover.

"Look in here?" he asked, pointing to the face and inside cover.

"Yup."

He toyed with the watch for several minutes. Then with his thumbnail he pried open the back, exposing the works.

"How about in here?"

Meyers hesitated, and shook his head. "Nope," he said, "I didn't look there."

Marc bounced to his feet. "Let's look. I'll go with you."

He fairly shoved Meyers out the door ahead of him. They entered a small room across the hall littered with a confusion of apparatus, a microscope, flood lights, a projector for viewing fingerprints.

Meyers laid the watch on a work bench and with a small, fine brush delicately covered the inside of the watch cover with dust. Lattice-like smudges appeared, etched on the bright metal. Meyers slid the watch into a projector, throwing a greatly enlarged image on the screen. Beside it, he placed the fingerprint card. He jabbed a cigarette into the corner of his mouth, flipped a match with his thumbnail, and squinted at the shadows.

"Got something here," he grunted. "I'd say them thumbprints are the same."

"Any doubts about it, Meyer?"

He shrugged. "Some, from a quick look. Not much, though."

"Check it carefully. Don't destroy the evidence, and keep track of that watch."

"Oke."

Slowly Marc returned to Anderson's office, sank into his chair and clicked his heels on the edge of the desk.

"Would you believe it, Jerry, Meegan's prints were inside the back cover."

"You steal his watch?"

Marc shook his head. "No. It was picked up in the park. The park across from the Porter home."

"How come? What's it doin' there?"

"Don't you know?"

"Would I be askin' if I did?"

"Where's Meegan now?"

"Cripes, Jordan," barked Anderson impatiently, "how should I know? Do you?"

"Yes, roughly. He's in either of two places—heaven or hell! I'd bet on the latter."

"What? You mean he's dead?"

"Not only dead; evaporated. He was burned up, not 'beyond recognition' as you so glibly reported to the newspapers, but burned up completely. Society need concern itself no longer with Mr. Meegan. His remains consist of two pieces of leather from his shoes, his corset stays, and the junk you see in that paper."

"Jordan, you're stark, raving mad! Crazy! You got hallucinations."

Marc grinned at him. "You're repetitious, Jerry. In a rut. You said that before. The fact remains, Meegan's dead."

"You've no proof. You can't convince me, or anybody else."

Marc shrugged. "The world's better off. It's no consequence to me, unless the murderer of Meegan also disposed of a couple of good friends of mine!"

Anderson's fist came down on the desk with a crash. His cheeks puffed with impatience.

"Jordan," he snapped, "I've heard enough! I got work to do. Beat it!"

"Thanks for the use of the hall, Jerry. 'Bye."

14

"Enjoyed the show, Marc, but where're we going now?" asked Nora idly. They were driving leisurely through the soft moonlit night.

"Oh," replied Marc, "I thought we might wind up the evening at the Purple Pot."

Nora gasped. "The Purple Pot! Why, Marc. I didn't know— I mean, I didn't think you ever went there, since—"

"Since the night last summer when I made an ass of myself, beat up the barkeep and spent the night in jail? I don't. Haven't been there since. Tonight I have a special reason."

Nora watched him from the corners of her eyes, a puzzled frown wrinkling her nose.

"What's special about it?"

"You'll see." Marc grinned at her. "I won't get drunk. I want you along to keep an eye on me!"

Nora patted his hand gently and laid her head for a moment on his shoulder.

"Don't be silly!" More seriously, she continued, "What are you going for? Really?"

He drove a block in silence.

"Investigations," he said.

"Oh!" said Nora, pouting. She flounced into the far corner of the seat and scowled in mock anger. "Don't you ever forget your investigations? Even with me?"

"Not this one! Not for long. It's too peculiar."

"You're a worry worm. What can you possibly expect to learn at the Purple Pot?"

"Strange things turn up in strange places," replied Marc evasively. "We arrive. Let's go see."

The low thump of music came from the rambling building. It was set apart by a carefully tended lawn on one side and a parking lot on the other. Marc found a vacant space for the Ford.

A waiter stopped abruptly as they entered the dimly lit, smoke-filled room.

"Mr. Jordan!" he exclaimed. "Ain't see you since—ain't seen you for quite a spell."

Marc grinned a friendly greeting. "Hello, Dan. Any place for us to sit?"

"Pretty busy, but we'll fix you up." He glanced around the room. "Over here."

He led the way to the far side where an unsteady couple were trying to fall into their wraps.

"Fine, Dan. As far away from that blasted orchestra as possible."

Dan leaned intimately over Marc's shoulder. "Confidentially, Mr. Jordan, it drives me nuts. Wasn't fer the dough these drunks lay out, I'd get me a job on yer railroad."

"Then you *would* be nuts!"

"Mebbe. What'll you have? You usta always take—"

"Beer!" interposed Marc hurriedly.

"Yes, sir. And the young lady?"

"I'll have beer too," replied Nora.

The waiter left to fill their order and she continued, "I don't like this place, Marc. Too rough and noisy. Bad associations."

"That's right. Thanks, Dan."

Dan plumped the bottles on the table. "That be all?"

"Dan," said Marc slowly, toying with his glass, "I'm curious about one of your customers. Chap that comes here often. He's short, heavy-set, with a thick face, and the lobe of his left ear missing."

"Oh, him? Sure. He's in here pretty near every night. Looks like a movie goon."

"Seen him lately?"

"Come to think about it, don't think he's been in fer a coupla nights now."

"Does he have any pals?"

"Seen him drink with the boys onct in a while. Not very often. Mostly he takes it alone, or with that there—that girl friend of his'n."

"She's a regular customer too, I suppose."

"Yeah."

"Point her out to me."

Dan stepped away from the booth and scanned the room. Shaking his head, he returned.

"Ain't here. Will be, I expect. Stick around."

"What's she look like?"

"Pink hair. Yeah, pink! Lotsa goo on her face. She bulges good where she should, bad where she shouldn't. Too much night work, I expect. Musta been real pretty, 'bout twenty years ago."

Marc chuckled and shot an amused glance at Nora. Her lips turned down distastefully.

"A vivid description, Dan. I know what you mean."

"I'll tell ya if she comes in."

"Better yet—I don't suppose she's proud?"

Dan snorted. "Proud? Her?"

"Bring her over here. I'd like to meet her. I'll buy her a drink."

Dan's face twisted into a disapproving scowl. He stared questioningly at Nora.

"Mr. Jordan, sir," he said, coughing apologetically, "I always did admire your sense, when you was sober. You figger this—you figger she'd be a good influence on your nice girl friend?"

Marc laughed loudly and squeezed Nora's hand.

"Quit worrying, Dan. Nora understands. This is in the line of business. Only don't you mention it."

A relieved grin spread over Dan's face.

"Right, sir," he said.

"So," said Nora, "that's why you wanted to come here. You're looking for—what's his name? Meegan."

Marc nodded. "And I'll be completely flabbergasted if I find him."

"Why?"

"Either I'm crazy, or he's dead."

Nora gasped. "And you think—but there's been nothing in the papers! And if he died naturally, you certainly wouldn't be looking for him."

"Smart girl. He died unnaturally. So unnaturally that no one will believe he died at all."

"I don't understand. How can that be?"

An apologetic cough interrupted her. Dan stood beside the booth.

"Here she is, sir." He jerked his head toward a short, plump woman at his side. Straggly hair, straying from under a round hat perched on the back of her head, was undeniably pink, tapering to a gray-brown mixture at the roots. Her face was flabby and soft, as were her orange-tipped fingers. A small, brilliantly tinted mouth was pursed, and wide eyes stared at Marc suspiciously. The eyes were remarkable; of such pale blue that Marc felt the shock of looking at a ghost. He scrambled to his feet.

"Good evening, Miss—ah—"

"Donovan. Trixie Donovan." Her rich, throaty voice contrasted surprisingly with her appearance.

"Miss Donovan. It's a pleasure to meet you. Join us in a drink?"

The blank eyes slowly narrowed. "You buyin'?"

"Of course."

"Take a free drink any time," she said with a smug grin, plumping her prominent hips onto the bench across the table. "Who's yer gal friend?"

"I beg your pardon. Miss Donovan, Miss O'Conner."

"Howja do?" she ogled Nora frankly. "Nice face, girlie. I'da beat yer looks once, but I wisht I had yer years. You'd do better to wear a uplift brassiere. Get them breasts up in the air." She put her hands under her own ample bosom, and heaved.

Nora flushed scarlet. "Thank you, I'm satisfied!"

Marc gulped a mouthful of beer, and nearly strangled. He coughed uncontrollably for many seconds.

Trixie transferred her pale gaze to him.

"What'sa matter. Got the heaves?"

"Sorry," he replied, mopping his flushed face with his handkerchief. "I do that once in a while."

"Where's that drink? Gotta cigarette?"

Marc shook one out for her, and crooked a finger at Dan.

"Take Miss Donovan's order, Dan. Anything she wants."

"Anything?"

"That's what I said."

"Double Scotch, sonny boy. Nothin' on the side."

She tapped the cigarette on the table and stuck it in the corner of her mouth.

"I ain't accustomed," she said, exhaling smoke as she talked, "Mr.— What's yer name?"

"Jordan."

"Mr. Jordan. I ain't accustomed to such sociability, 'specially when a guy's got his gal along. What's it mean?"

"I'm interested in interesting people, Miss Donovan," he replied affably. "I've heard of you, and wanted to meet you."

"Sounds fishy." Trixie's eyes narrowed. "What've you heard? Who from?"

"From a friend of mine."

Dan returned, set a glass on the table and turned away. Trixie rapped imperiously.

"Stick around!" She took a swallow from the glass, gasped, and drained it. "Fill'r up. What friend?"

"A man who knew a gentleman named Meegan. Fact, I was hoping to meet him too. Have you seen him?"

Trixie blew the ash from the end of her cigarette and stared at the glowing end. Deliberately, she looked at Marc.

"How come yer hangin' around me and Meegan?"

Marc shrugged. "I told you. I collect histories of colorful people."

"Colorful, you crazy? You call gettin' kicked outa the movies on account of dirty politics colorful? An' bouncin' around, moochin' a free meal an' a drink, datin' all kinds o' men, you call that colorful? Nuts!"

"Depends on the definition of the word," said Marc dryly. He was interrupted by Dan. Trixie half drained the glass he placed before her.

"Yeah!" she muttered.

"Is Calumet your home?"

"Home? Ain't got none. Born here, 'f that's what you mean." She sloshed the liquor around in her glass, then emptied it. "Can you imagine? I had a mother! Yes, sir, jus' like you'n this sweet gal. Kinda pit'ful, ain't it?"

"So you've come home to retire."

"Retire? Huh! Gals like me don't retire. We jus' get unemployed!"

"What did you do in Hollywood?"

"Acted, you dope! Damn good actin', too. I was gonna be a star. Then a director fired me."

"Did you know Meegan there?" asked Marc softly.

"Heck no. He picked me up in Los Angeles." She tilted her head slyly. "Only I really picked him up. Fine gen'leman, Slatsy is. Mighty fine." She suddenly stiffened. "Wha's he got to do with it? I'm the one with color, ain't I?"

"Decidedly! You didn't say when you saw him last."

She propped her chin on her fist sorrowfully. "Two—three days now, I ain't seen him. I'm gettin' lonesome. What I need's a drink! Hey, you!" She gestured to Dan, holding her glass upside down.

Dan approached, a questioning look on his face. Marc nodded.

"Same thing," said Trixie, handing the glass to Dan.

"Another friend of mine took a fling at the movies. Maybe you knew her. Cynthia Porter."

"Cynthia?" Trixie twitched, and with some difficulty focused her pale eyes on Marc. "Oughta. Roomed with her. My pal! Me, I hits her fer a little dough, fer old times' sake, 'n she brushes me off. But we gotta angle! Her kid's got lotsa bucks. The Old Man's been generous, the sap!"

"Cynthia was married for the first time in the West."

Trixie, starting to work on the glass Dan delivered, shook her head emphatically.

"Nope," she said.

Marc's voice was edged with surprise. "But she had a daughter. Miriam was born in Los Angeles, I'm told."

Trixie pressed her shoulders against the seat back.

Her head weaved slightly and she glared at Marc.

"Mr.—what's yer name?—Mr. Jordan! Ain't yer ma told you? Don't hafta be married to have a kid."

Nora gulped. Her face blanched and she stared aghast at Marc.

"But," he insisted, "she says she was married."

Trixie nodded. "Sure. Was gonna. But her man was bumped off by an auto first."

"You're sure?"

"Sure I'm sure!" Trixie bristled. "Di'n' I tell ya I lived with her?"

"This 'angle' you speak of, is Mr. Meegan helping you?"

"That's my business!"

"Is Miss Miriam more free with her money, for old times' sake?"

"Tha's my business too." She picked up her glass and squinted into it. "Three double Scotch. Shix drinksh. Tha's 'nuff." She slammed the glass on the table and stared balefully at Marc. "Yer pumpin' me! Yer trying to get me drunk an' pump me. Won' work, see? Know when to quit. Coupla more drinksh 'n I'll be drunk, see? When I'm drunk I talk too much, see? Well, I won' get drunk, see? Won't tell ya none o' my business. Yer too damned curious."

With difficulty, she struggled to her feet and stood unsteadily, clutching the side of the booth.

"G'bye. Thanksh for the drinksh. Shee ya 'round."

She took a step away, turned back and grabbed again for the booth post, peering at Nora.

"Get a uplift, girlie. Get 'em up where they show. Do ya lo'sa good."

Away she went, weaving starboard to port and back. Customers who saw her coming ducked, others were bumped. Grimly, Marc watched her vanish through the door. Nora sputtered.

"Of all the disgusting exhibitions! You're to blame, Marc Jordan, deliberately getting her drunk. It was absolutely indecent. If that's the kind of woman you associate with, I'm glad I found out!"

"Whoa! Slow down. She got herself drunk. And see the amazing bit of information we netted."

"Huh! I wouldn't believe a word she says. The filthy, lying cheat!"

"Maybe life's been tough for her. I believe her."

"Oh, you! You turn my stomach!"

Slowly Marc turned to her. "Miriam's illegitimate. It's been kept mighty quiet. Did you know it?"

Nora shrank from his anger. "No!"

"You're intimate with Miriam. Did she ever wistfully mention her infancy, or her father?"

"No."

"Did she ever say she'd like to visit California?"

"No."

"Ever show any interest in her birthplace?"

"No."

"Why? That's unnatural. How many, many things it explains."

"You're crazy!"

"Sure! Everyone else in Calumet thinks so, too. Drink your beer."

"It's warm. I've no taste for it."

"Then let's go."

"That," said Nora icily, "is your first sensible remark. This place gives me the creeps."

Marc signaled to Dan, who was hovering nearby. He grinned uncertainly.

"The lady picked up a load, but fast!" he said.

"She's had practice," replied Marc, dropping a bill on the table. "Thanks, Dan."

"Come again, Mr. Jordan."

"He will not," snapped Nora.

Stepping into the open, both sucked deep breaths of the refreshing air. Wordlessly, they climbed into the car.

Cautiously working his way out of the crowded lot, Marc hesitated at the street entrance. A faint wail increased with steady crescendo to a hair-stiffening shriek. With a flashing red spotlight staining the darkness, an ambulance careened past.

15

Stepping into the bright sunshine after a hurried lunch, Marc strolled along Main Street toward the railroad building. He usually walked to lunch. His long body needed exercise to offset the sedentary office routine.

He was vaguely conscious that two trim figures ahead of him were familiar. Quickening his step, he soon caught them.

"Beautiful day," he said with brilliant originality.

"Why, hello, Marc," said Cynthia and Miriam in unison.

"Wish I'd known you lovely ladies were in town. I hate to eat alone. We could have had lunch together."

Miriam laughed. "It'd be a waste of time. Mother's on a shopping jag. There's no stopping her."

Cynthia frowned. "It's most discouraging. There isn't a decent yard of drape material in town. I must find some."

"It's really a wonderful excuse, Marc. The fire, you know. Mother's wanted new drapes for a year."

Cynthia stopped in front of an elaborate store entrance.

"Let's try Altmyer's, Miriam," she suggested. "They may have something."

"Come along, Marc?" asked Miriam.

Marc chuckled. "No thanks! Shopping's a brand of torture I assiduously avoid."

"Smart man. 'Bye."

Thoughtfully, Marc watched them enter the store and head straight for an elevator. He glanced at his watch and made a quick calculation. One-thirty. Don Porter would still be at Rotary. He stepped to the curb, flagged a cab and directed the driver to the Tenth Avenue park.

"Yes *sir,*" said the cabby affably. "Lotsa guys wouldn't take you clean out there, mister. Too far out, they says. No money in it. Now me, I like to get up and go. All the time drivin' in traffic, it gets me. Hard work, you know it? I like some fresh air onct in a while. You live out Tenth Avenoo, mister?"

"No," replied Marc. "Just friends of mine."

"They're lucky. Beautiful homes out there. Wisht I was rich and could have me a fancy place. Well, inna coupla months my hack'll be paid off. Then me 'n the missus're gonna get a place out. Not so fancy mebbe, but some land where I can grow nasturtiums and pole beans. Brother, how I like pole beans!"

The jolly cabby chattered constantly, requiring only grunts from Marc for incentive. Circling the park, he twisted his chin over his shoulder.

"Where ya wanna get off, Mister?"

"This will be fine." Marc paid the driver and stepped onto the grass. "Thanks."

He walked through the park and stopped across from the Porters'. The rubble had been completely cleared from the garage. The bare concrete floor afforded nothing more than a parking place. Harrison, booted to the thighs, was busily scrubbing a big sedan. Marc strolled over to him.

"Hello, Harrison. Anyone home?"

"How do, Mr. Jordan, sir. I'm sorry, but everyone is away."

"That's too bad. Even Aunt Sarah?"

"Yes sir. Today's a big day for her. Her Bible Society meets today."

"Expect anyone soon?"

"Mrs. Porter and Miss Miriam went shopping. I expected them before now. I'm to meet Mr. Porter with the car at five."

"I see. Mind if I go in and wait?"

"Not at all, sir; go right in."

"I'll bother Mrs. H. and keep her from working."

"Afraid you won't, sir. She's gone to market."

"This place's practically a morgue, eh, Harrison?"

Harrison smiled weakly. "Practically, sir."

Marc casually crossed the lawn and mounted the steps to the veranda. Once he was inside, his casualness vanished. With lightning steps and a feeling of guilt, he bounded up the stairs to the second floor. On the landing he paused to get his bearings, then darted into the room occupied by Cynthia and Porter.

It was large, extending half the length of the house across the front. Twin beds jutted from the inside wall, with a combination book shelf and chest between. A dressing table faced the outside wall with a window on each side. A large, masculine dresser stood in the outside corner. Opposite, over the front entrance, were two doors. One led to a bathroom; the other gave into a large closet.

Marc started on the bed table. He felt through all the drawers and pulled out all the books, searching behind them. He worked swiftly, but with care, returning everything to position as he had found it. Finding nothing, he moved to the corner chest. He pawed through the drawers of socks, shirts, underwear. One drawer contained a jumble of male junk. The lower two held blankets. He removed each, running his hands between the folds.

Suddenly he stepped to the window. Harrison was methodically continuing his automotive ablutions. It would be most embarrassing to be surprised. Marc estimated the route and distance to the family bathroom leading off the hall. A hurry call of nature could be used as an excuse if necessary.

Finishing with the chest, he continued around the room to the dressing table. This had only two small drawers, one on each side. One contained neatly rolled hose, the other odds and ends of feminine beauty equipment.

The closet came next. He whipped through the rows of clothes hung on hangers. Several traveling cases were tucked into a dark corner on the floor. These he snapped open, and felt through all the pockets.

Stretching to his full six feet two, he examined the shelf above the clothes rack and fumbled through several boxes. At the back was a large bundle, two feet long and a foot in diameter. He tore enough of the paper wrapping to see that it contained cotton. Cynthia was old-fashioned enough to do quilting.

Puzzled, he stepped back and surveyed the room. As an afterthought, he ran his hands over the beds and under the mattresses. Checking Harrison again, he went into the bathroom.

The elaborate, chrome-plated medicine cabinet contained the bottles and tubes found in all medicine cabinets. To the right, a closet was used for linen and more bulky bathroom supplies. Tucked into a corner, under a pile of towels, his hand struck a box. Curiously, he pulled it into the open.

A candy box, it contained several chocolate creams, and a small package labeled: "Rat Poison!" This Marc weighed in his hand, closed, and returned to its hiding place.

Stepping into the hall, he faced the end of the house toward the garage, and hesitated. Straight ahead was the bath, to the right Dolly's room, to the left Miriam's, and behind him Aunt Sarah's. He selected Miriam's next. Despite the scorched window casing, the freshly puttied glass, and the absence of curtains, the room had an air of fluffiness. Tony's picture grinned at him from the top of a chiffonier and beside it the handsome portrait of Karl Snyder. A ridiculous kewpie doll sat demurely between lace pillows at the head of the bed. A chintz-covered chair and a dainty dressing table completed the furnishings.

Marc started methodically through the chiffonier. In a bottom drawer, under a pile of frilly lingerie, his hand struck a hard object. He fished it out and, untangling a silk pantie, stared with a surge of satisfaction mixed with dread at a flat, wicked, snub-nosed gun.

He thought fast. Dropping the gun into his pocket, he ran to Porter's room and pulled a heavy quilt from a drawer in the chest. Swiftly he stepped to the closet and snatched the bulky roll of cotton batting. With this plunder he went into the hall bathroom.

Undoing the wrapping paper from the roll of cotton, he laid it in the bathtub. He selected two hand towels from the linen closet. One he folded and refolded into a pad a few inches square. This he laid on top of the cotton. First turning on a water faucet in the wash bowl, he pulled the gun from his pocket and loosely wrapped the second towel around the gun and his lower arm. He pressed the muzzle against the linen pad and with his free hand wadded the quilt thickly over his whole arm and the cotton roll. Thus prepared, he pulled the trigger.

A sharp but muffled crack reverberated from the tile walls. With the speed and sureness of a cat, he freed his hand from the blanket, grabbed the blackened and smoldering linen pad and doused it under the running water, then wrapped it in the other towel and stuffed it into his pocket.

The blanket he folded as he had found it. The click of the door and a step on the stair chilled his spine.

"Mr. Jordan, sir?"

Tensely, Marc absorbed several deep breaths before answering. Then he opened the door a crack.

"Yes, Harrison, what is it? I'm up here."

"Heard a strange, sharp noise, sir. I wondered if you were all right."

"Had a hurry call, Harrison," replied Marc, struggling to maintain a jocular tone. "Banged my knee on the stair coming up."

"Oh. All right, sir. I'm sorry."

Peeking through the crack in the door, Marc heaved a sigh of relief when Harrison turned and retraced his steps. After waiting until he heard the front door click again, he unwound the roll of cotton. A black hole, decreasing as the roll unwound, punctured each layer. Near the center, the hole failed to penetrate, and Marc's probing fingers located a warm chunk of lead. Disentangling the strands of cotton, he popped it into his vest pocket.

With trembling fingers, now clumsy in haste, he rewound the cotton and tucked it back on the closet shelf. The blanket he put away, and the gun, after a careful polishing, he returned to Miriam's chiffonier.

He made a hurried reconnaissance, pushed open the bathroom window to dispel gun fumes, and trotted to the first floor, where he picked up the telephone and called a cab. Then, packing his pipe, he nonchalantly lit it and descended the veranda steps.

"I don't believe I'll wait any longer," he said.

Harrison nodded. "Right, sir."

"Harrison," Marc paused and sucked on his pipe, "I've changed my mind. Will you do me a favor?"

"If I can, sir."

"You can. Please don't tell any of the family I called this afternoon."

"Of course, sir, if you wish."

"I do. I'll explain later. Thanks, Harrison."

"Yes sir."

Marc strolled toward the street, which he reached as the cab drove up. He gave the driver his home address.

In his room, Marc shucked his coat onto the bed, swept away a litter of books from his desk and spread out a piece of blank. paper. From the drawer he picked two small boxes and a jeweler's double lens eyeglass which he laid beside the paper.

On one corner of the paper, he wrote: "Porter." Under this he laid the recently acquired slug. He then wrote "Miriam" and "Meegan," and placed similar slugs from each of the two small boxes under each name.

He inserted the glass under his eyelid like a monocle and peered at the evil pieces of metal. He examined each in turn, swinging his head back and forth. With the point of a pencil he rolled them about. He was thus intently occupied when a jarring rap on the door caused him to jump and drop the eyeglass.

16

Marc retrieved the fallen glass, hurriedly shoved papers over the bullet display and stepped to the door. A tall, embarrassed cop stood in the hall.

"Hello, Pete," said Marc. "Come in."

Apologetically whirling his cap, Pete entered.

"What is it?" continued Marc.

"Mr. Jordan, could you come down to headquarters?"

"A pinch?" asked Marc jokingly.

"Not exactly." Pete hesitated. "I ain't got no warrant. But Anderson'd like to see you."

"Why?"

"Couldn't say. Just told me to bring you in. Here's about the last place I figgered to find you, this time o' day."

"Then it *is* a pinch!" replied Marc dryly. "Sit down, Pete. Be with you in a minute." He pointed to a chair at the end of the room, as far from his desk as possible.

Returning to the desk, and shielding his actions with his body, Marc selected three envelopes, marked them "A," "B," and "C." Writing a corresponding letter beside the names on the paper, he popped a bullet into each envelope, sealed them and tucked them into his pocket.

Then he walked to the door.

"Let's go," he said.

Pete joined him and they descended to the street.

"Shall I drive my car?" asked Marc.

"Better ride with me."

"Don't trust me, eh? Okay, Peter, you're in charge. No idea what Anderson wants?"

Pete shook his head. "Nope."

"Wouldn't tell me if you did, would you?"

Pete didn't answer. They drove to headquarters in silence and he led the way directly to the office.

Anderson crouched behind his desk, his flushed face more flushed than usual, his cigar stump tilted at an angry angle. He stared owlishly at Marc.

"Where ya been hidin'?" he demanded.

"Hiding? Why? And from whom?"

"From me. And why, is what I wanta know."

"What makes you think I've been hiding?"

"You wasn't at your office or any of your usual places."

"I was home. Is that hiding? And how do you know my 'usual' places?"

"I got connections." Anderson's grin was mirthless.

"Suppose you answer some questions." Marc struggled to control his anger. "What's the reason for dragging me in on the arm of a cop?"

"I'm suspicious of you, Jordan. What you been up to?"

"Please be more specific."

"You were at the Purple Pot last night," said Anderson flatly.

"That's no crime, is it?"

"Depends. Who were you with?"

"My fiancée, Miss Nora O'Connor," replied Marc.

"Who else?"

"We had a pleasant conversation with an interesting woman, Miss Trixie Donovan."

"Yah! You admit it!"

"Of course. Why not?"

"Did you know, my smart friend, that Miss Donovan was shot last night? Right after talkin' to you! Darn near killed."

Marc stiffened. He sank into a chair and raised his feet to the desk.

"You don't say," he murmured. "Amazing. Who did the shooting?"

"That," growled Anderson truculently, "is what you're gonna tell me."

"Rats, Jerry!" Marc shrugged impatiently. "Be reasonable. Do you think I did?"

"Well, no. But I'll bet ya know who did, and why."

"What're you betting on?"

"A hunch."

"Jerry, you playing hunches too? My, my."

"You had some reason fer lookin' up this bag. What was it? What'd you talk about?"

"History. Fascinating history."

"Spill it."

Marc knocked the dottle from his pipe and stared coldly at Anderson.

"I've been trying for six weeks. You're too stupid to listen."

"Jordan," Anderson's voice rasped harshly, "I got grounds to book you on suspicion. Start talkin'."

"You really want to know, do you?"

"You're right. I do."

"Murder, Jerry. Remember? Three of 'em."

"You think this dame's in it?"

"I don't think; I know. She's the next victim. Someone's a bad shot, or she'd be dead—not that it matters much."

Anderson sighed and some of his bluster evaporated. "Start back a ways. I'm just a cop."

Marc leaned forward and punched holes in the air with the stem of his pipe.

"O.K." he said. "Listen: Dolly Porter died. Accident, you say. Ted Arthur died with her. I say Dolly was murdered in cold blood. Slats Meegan's dead. Cremated. I can't prove that except circumstantially, but dead he is. Again murder. Now Trixie Donovan's shot. Why? Because they all knew something! Something mighty important."

"I'll ask it, Jordan," growled Anderson. "What did they know?"

Marc leaned back and stared at the ceiling. He shook his head.

"I suppose you salvaged a bullet from Miss Donovan's almost worthless carcass?"

Glaring at him, Anderson laid a sheet of paper on the desk. He dumped the contents of a small pasteboard box, a pellet of lead, on the paper and pointed to it with a jerk.

"You interested?"

"Very." Marc leaned forward and glanced at it. From his pocket he selected an envelope and slid it toward Anderson.

"Look that over," he said calmly. "Compare it with yours."

Puzzled and suspicious, Anderson tore open the envelope and placed a second pellet beside the first.

"Where'd you get this?" he demanded.

"Look at it," replied Marc. "Then maybe I'll tell you."

"You'll tell me, son!"

Anderson wheeled around to a microscope standing on the wide window ledge at his back. He slid the pellets onto the stand and toyed with the eye piece. For five minutes, his stertorous breathing and the gurgle of Marc's pipe were the only sounds in the room. Then Anderson turned back, removed and slowly polished his thick glasses, and peered at Marc.

"They look alike," he grunted. "Now, Mr. Jordan, is when you tell me where you got that slug—or else!"

Marc sprang to his feet and crowded behind Anderson. Folding his long frame at right angles, he squinted through the microscope.

"Just checking you, Jerry," he said dryly, returning to his chair. "All right, I'll tell you. But first," a wide grin spread across his face, "I want immunity for turning state's evidence!"

"Huh?" demanded Anderson. "Immunity from what?"

"Housebreaking. I did a little job."

"I thought so. Had a idea you were foolin' around with trouble. Talk!"

"Ever hear of Slats Meegan, Jerry?"

"I'm listenin'."

"The tin cash box I showed you *was* a cash box. Literally. Belonged to Mr. Meegan, as you proved. I found it in his room, full of cash!"

"Well, well. About two days ago, eh? Roomin' house entered on Eastern Avenue. So you're the porch climber!"

"Don't oil up your handcuffs till you hear the rest. Yes, I entered Meegan's room. I found the cash box, among other things, with two-three thousand dollars in it. The money's in Meegan's suitcase. I didn't take it. But in the box, under the money, was a poster: 'Wanted for Murder—Slats Meegan.' The same poster you showed me. Under the poster was a small box of gun shells, with one slug. A souvenir. You're now gazing upon that slug!"

Anderson's face was a study. The impact of this news was slow to penetrate.

"Meegan's, huh?" he said. "Come from Meegan's gun. But you say he's dead?"

"I do, and he is. The bullet came from his gun, but he didn't fire it, naturally." Marc laid a second envelope on the desk. "Now look at this," he said.

Anderson weighed the envelope in his hand and glowered at Marc. Slowly he turned again to his microscope, peeked through it, and wheeled back.

"I suppose this slug's gotta history too. Where'd you get it?"

"Out of the cushion in the Porter davenport. Remember? Miriam was shot at, a short time ago."

"But we picked up Meegan, and he didn't have no gun."

Marc nodded. "You had your hands on the key man in this case and let him go. Of course he didn't have a gun. He ditched it under a bush in the park. I had a man tailing him. He spotted Meegan hunting for something there several nights later. The mark of the gun was still clear in the dirt when Klutz showed me the place."

"You gotta theory why Meegan shot through the window?"

"Not only why he shot, but why he missed. He didn't have to miss, you know." Marc tossed the last envelope to Anderson. "One more, Jerry. Cast your bright eyes on that."

"You're gettin' in a rut, Jordan," growled Anderson sarcastically. "This match the others?"

"It does."

"I'll take your word for it." He scratched a match viciously across the desk top and lit his drooping cigar. "I'm holdin' my breath!"

Marc rose and slowly strode the length of the office and back.

"This one's most interesting! I called at the Porters' this P.M. No one home but Harrison. Finding it necessary to go upstairs, I just happened to find a wicked gun in a dresser drawer. The last bullet came from that gun."

"The same gun? Meegan's gun? At the Porters'?"

"Clever of you, Jerry. Think over the odyssey of that gun. Meegan's undoubtedly. The slug in his cash box proves that. He used it to shoot at—and miss —Miss Miriam Porter, then hid it in the park. Now it bobs up as the weapon used to shoot Donovan. A surprising development. Why didn't I think of the possibility!"

"Maybe Meegan used it on his girl friend."

"Do you really think that Meegan, if living, would hide his gun in a drawer at the Porters'? That's where it is, or was an hour ago. How did it get there, then? Obviously it was removed from Meegan's dead body. Proof, to my mind, that Meegan was killed on the Porter property."

Anderson leaped to his feet, knocking his chair over backwards with a crash.

"I want that gun!" he barked. "Now!"

Marc held up a restraining hand. "Wait, Jerry. Wouldn't you rather have the person who killed Dolly, Ted, and Meegan?"

"If there's such a guy, yes."

"There is, believe me."

"That'll be someone at the Porters' who used the gat on the Donovan dame."

"Agreed. But how do you propose to prove who that is? It could be any one of half a dozen. I'll bet my reputation and a year's pay that the instant you barge in, the Porter clan, to a man, will close up like clams."

"How'd you do it? Not that I give a rap!"

"I'd slip up on them. Go in the back way."

"And you've a nice, neat, tidy, clever plan, no doubt."

"No doubt."

17

"Where are you going, Marc?" Tony touched the glowing dash board lighter to his cigarette and inhaled a deep draught of smoke.

"The Porter house," replied Marc laconically.

"The Porters'?" Tony's head snapped around in surprise. "What's up?"

"Tony," said Marc, gripping the wheel and concentrating on the road, "how long have we been friends?"

Tony's surprise grew. "A good many years. The best damn team of dish washers the University of Michigan ever saw!"

"Right. I think a lot of you. Don't forget it. I don't want to lose your friendship. That's why I want you along tonight."

"If I were working in my office, I'd say you're in a state of mind. What's gnawing at you?"

"A nasty scene's coming up. You've attachments at the Porters'. I want you on the ground to get the straight of it."

"What in the world are you hinting at?"

Marc drove in silence for a block. "Maybe I'm wrong. You just listen. Besides, I need help. Will you?"

"Help? If I can."

"I want to talk to the family in one piece. I banked on one of Don's idiosyncrasies: he insists they have dinner together. Nora dropped in on the pretext of asking Miriam about a benefit bridge party. She called me. They're all there. You can, without attracting attention, stay close to Miriam. Do so! Watch her, and whatever happens, keep your mouth shut."

Tony, his boyish face pale, his eyes blank and strained, twisted sideways and stared at Marc.

"I don't like the sound of this," he said deliberately. "Is Miriam in danger?"

Marc gritted his teeth. "Maybe, a little. Anyway, stay close to her. Don't let her leave the room alone."

"Why? Don't be so blasted mysterious."

"It's better this way, Tony. You might drop sand in the gears if you knew too much."

"Remember, pal," Tony punctuated each word, "there's just one person I'm looking after—Miriam!"

His face gray, Marc nodded. "I know. Well, here we go. Let me do the talking."

He turned into the Porter drive and stopped. Harrison answered the door in response to his knock.

"Anyone home, Harrison?"

"Yes, sir, Mr. Jordan—Doctor Bodine. Come in, please."

Cynthia appeared in the door to the dining room as they stepped into the hall.

"Who is it, Harrison? . . . Why, Marc, Tony, how nice!" A smile hid a trace of annoyance at the interruption. "We're just having dessert and coffee. Won't you join us? Nora's here too."

Tony withdrew into the background and Marc shook his head.

"Thanks, Cynthia. We've had dinner. There are some things I'd like to talk over with all of you. Could you spare a few minutes after dinner?"

The blood drained slowly from Cynthia's face, and the narrowing slits of her eyes betrayed increasing annoyance, still masked by a friendly smile.

"Of course, Marc. Anything important?"

"Rather. I'd like you all present."

"Harrison, take Mr. Jordan and Doctor Bodine into the living room. We'll be with you in a minute, Marc."

Tony, sinking into the davenport, tapped a cigarette viciously on the arm.

"You're a heel, Jordan," he growled. "A discourteous heel."

Spraddle-legged, Marc thrust his hands into his pockets and glared at him.

"For once, I agree with your diagnosis. As Pop said when he swung the strap, this hurts me more than it does you!" He squatted on a beautiful, uncomfortable, carved mahogany chair placed before the fireplace and slowly twisted a lock of hair around his forefinger.

Soon, dinner over, members of the family drifted in. Aunt Sarah, grim and silent, tramped across the room to her rocker by the window and picked up her knitting. Only once did she tilt her head and glare at Marc over the top of her glasses.

A sober-faced Tony met Miriam at the door. He squeezed her hand and led her to the davenport. Nora followed and slipped quietly into a corner chair more or less out of sight. Cynthia paused at the door.

"I'll be there in a moment, Marc," she said brightly, darting up the stairs.

Joel, bored and sneering, slunk in and dropped into a chaise longue. Porter, working over his molars with a toothpick and making hissing sounds with his tongue, brought up the rear.

"Quite a gathering," he said gruffly, glancing around the room. "A social call?"

Marc smiled weakly. "Not very social, Don. I want to discuss some matters of importance with you." He looked quickly at Miriam, whose wide eyes were questioningly on him. Cynthia returned, sought a big chair in a remote corner.

"Now," she said, "we're all here. What is it, Marc? Let's have a drink first. Harrison, the bar."

Harrison, moving swiftly and silently, wheeled a portable bar in from the pantry, and added a bowl of ice cubes.

"Every man for himself," said Porter, filling a glass. During the ensuing confusion, there was a rough knock at the door. A few seconds later the squat form of Anderson, his face dark and truculent, his hat riding the back of his head, loomed in the doorway.

Porter wheeled. "What the—" he demanded, then turned back to Marc, a flush of anger mounting to his ruddy cheeks. "What goes on, Jordan? Why the police department?"

"Relax, folks," interrupted Anderson. "Jordan's got something on his chest. I wanta hear. Step on it, Jordan. I'm a busy man."

Marc glanced quickly around the room. Each occupant, in his own way, showed surprise, and something akin to fear. Cynthia held her glass halfway to her lips. Miriam's startled eyes jumped from Tony to Marc to Anderson and back. Porter sputtered, Aunt Sarah knitted and Joel gnawed his fingernails.

"Relax yourself, Jerry," said Marc quietly. He turned to Porter. "Sorry, Don. I've important things to say. It won't be pleasant, to make a colossal understatement, but necessary."

"Well, get on with it," snapped Porter. "I'm busy too."

"Yes." Marc squirmed on the hard chair. Doubts assailed him. He found it impossible at the moment to look Miriam in the eye. He held up his pipe. "Mind, Cynthia?"

At her nod, he slowly loaded it, and walked to the end of the room where he stood facing them.

"To start with," he said deliberately, "a word of apology. You're friends of mine. I've snooped around your private lives. Sorry, but it seemed necessary. I'm selfish. I want you all to hear the justification of my actions."

He paused, shivered as though about to leap into ice water, and continued.

"Let's go back. You know the main points. Many details you may not know, or have forgotten. A very pleasant evening some weeks ago, a dinner here and a party at the Ship's Hold ended in the tragic death of Ted and Dolly. An accident, the official report says."

"Marc," interrupted Miriam weakly, her handkerchief pressed to her lips, "is this necessary?"

He glanced sharply at her. "I'm afraid so." He walked to a window and gazed into the thickening twilight, turned back.

"Did you ever stop to think of the many hours in all our lives when our actions are unaccounted for? When we're doing things in places unknown, or unnoticed? Take the night of the party. I left Nora at her door, assuming that she went in and to bed. Did

she? She assumed when I left that I went home. Did I? When Tony left Miriam here, he too assumed she went in and to bed. Did you?"

Miriam gasped. "Of course!"

"But can you prove it?" Marc snapped the words. "No! When Jane bid Ted Arthur good night, she assumed he was going home. Did he? He wound up a mangled corpse beside the railroad track! When Dolly, suffering from an attack of indigestion, left Karl, he had every right to expect that she'd be safe in bed in fifteen minutes. Was she? Her pretty party dress was soon a blood-soaked rag and her body torn to shreds!"

"Jordan, you fiend!" Porter's voice was a menacing growl. Balefully he rose from his chair.

"Hold on, Don." Marc advanced, jabbing his pipe stem accusingly. "Can you prove where you were? We left you at the Ship's Hold. Did you stay?"

"Yes," he replied defiantly, sinking back. "What're you driving at?"

"Just this—Dolly and Ted didn't die in an accident. They were murdered in cold blood!"

A moment of explosive silence followed this announcement. Cynthia's glass hit the hardwood floor with a shattering crash. Miriam swayed slightly, and Tony steadied her. The rest were marble statues.

"The sins of the fathers," cackled Sarah, resuming her knitting, "shall be visited upon the children unto the third and fourth generation."

Marc spun about.

"Sarah!" he exclaimed. "Have I overlooked something? I've neglected you."

"Jordan," snarled Porter, "you'd better be sure what you're saying! Inspector," he turned to Anderson, "must we listen to this drivel?"

Anderson shrugged. "Look, Mr. Porter, this guy's been drivin' me nuts for weeks with his yarn. Threatened to turn the whole thing over to the papers, if I didn't let him brace you first. Let'm rave. We can hang him later."

"That's it, eh?" said Porter. "Okay, Jordan. Dig yourself a hole."

"Thanks, Don," replied Marc dryly. "Let me tell you why it was murder and not an accident. Engineer Baxter states flatly that Dolly's car was standing on the crossing. But a car won't stand there, unless the brakes are set. So someone set the brakes."

"Ever hear of a person becoming frozen with fear, unable to move?" Tony's voice was low.

"If that were the only point in doubt, Tony," replied Marc slowly, "I'd agree. Lacking other evidence, I'd even guess that Ted was the lad who set the brakes. But he wasn't.

"The fireman saw a second car at the wreck. That car was Ted's. I've a picture, taken that night, of the tracks of his car in the mud to prove it. Yet we found his car parked out here in the street." Marc gestured toward the window. "I've another picture. It shows two sets of footprints: one leaving the car; one returning. They're different. The prints leaving the car are Ted's.

"Ted was outside the car when it was struck. I can prove that too. He died trying to get Dolly out!"

The silence was heavy with emotion. No one broke it. Marc looked at Miriam. Her eyes were those of a bird watching a snake.

"Miriam," he said, "Tony must've left you here soon after Dolly got home."

She winced as though struck. Tony's rosy cheeks turned the color of ice.

"Marc—" he choked.

"Shut up, Tony!"

"Marc!" Cynthia's voice was a wail. "What—"

"Cynthia," said Marc, turning to her, "you were here. Didn't you hear any commotion?"

She shook her head.

"How about you, Sarah?"

"The Lord made the night for rest, not sinning. That's what I use it for!"

"I see. Let's proceed. A week or so later, you were shot at, Miriam. Remember? The hole in the davenport's still there."

Fascinated, a half-dozen pairs of eyes stared at the rent.

"That puzzles me, Miriam. See if I have it straight. You sat for fifteen minutes, reading the paper. You got up, and the bullet thudded into the cushion. That right?"

Mutely she nodded.

"How strange! If some fiend meant to kill you, why fritter away fifteen minutes when you were a perfect target, and then shoot after you moved? Are you sure, Miriam," Marc stood before her and spoke slowly, "that it wasn't an act? Did you do the shooting, dash back here, and scream?"

Miriam swayed. "No—no—no!"

Cynthia and Porter were both on their feet.

"Marc, you despicable viper!" Cynthia snarled.

Anderson emitted a sneering chuckle. "Good show, Jordan. Keep it up."

Marc disregarded him. "Sit down, Don. And you, Cynthia. There's more. How unfortunate that none of you can account for your actions that night either! An elusive family. Let's suppose you didn't fake the scene. Then there's only one explanation, Miriam. No one intended to harm you. The shot was a warning. Why should someone need to warn you in such a melodramatic fashion?"

Her purple lips moved, but no sound came forth. Marc turned abruptly and took up a stand at the end of the room again.

Porter bit the end from a cigar with a crunch of his powerful jaws. He pointed it at Marc like a gun.

"Mighty insulting insinuations, Jordan," he snapped.

"Don," replied Marc, "this whole investigation's been most distasteful. But I've learned some things that point a finger of suspicion right at the end of your nose!"

Porter's jaw sagged. He jammed the cigar between his lips and sank back angrily.

"A few days of peace," continued Marc, "and then Miriam's kidnaped! Anderson thinks you were out painting the town. Were you, Miriam?"

She stared at the floor. "Do you think that too, Marc?"

"No," he replied, "I don't. You were kidnaped. But," he frowned at her, "why were you held only a few hours, then released? Why was no effort made to contact your family? The usual reason for kidnaping is money. Strange, isn't it?"

Slowly Miriam raised her eyes to his. "I don't know, Marc."

"I do! Again someone was trying to frighten you, and succeeded. Why Miriam? That's what I want to know. Why?"

Miriam buried her face in her hands and sobbed softly. Tony slipped his arm around her shoulders protectingly.

"Jordan," he said savagely, "lay off!"

"I won't lay off!" Marc's savagery matched his. "I'm going to get to the bottom of this, whoever it hurts. Three corpses are enough. I'll have no more if I can help it."

"Three?" demanded Porter, choking on a mouthful of smoke.

"Sorry," said Marc, "I run ahead. We come now to a shoddy figure—one Slats Meegan. Quite a versatile gentleman, Mr. Meegan. I'd like to have known him.

"Don, I talked you into engaging Thatcher to follow Meegan. I didn't tell you that I was more interested in which of your family Meegan was dealing with. Unfortunately, he always managed to give Thatcher's man the slip at critical times. Not that it matters much now," he added.

"Meegan and you, Cynthia, had a mutual friend, Miss Trixie Donovan. A colorful character. Remember her?"

Cynthia, rigid, her eyes slits in a blank mask, nodded slowly.

"I roomed with her in Hollywood."

"Seen her lately?"

"She borrowed some money from me."

"I see. I heard it somewhat differently. But to get back to Meegan—" Marc hesitated a moment and then turned to Porter. "Don, tell me, why did you show such a burst of speed in clearing up the mess in your garage after the fire?"

"Huh?" he said in surprise. "Why, just to get it cleaned up. Can't stand a mess around."

"That the only reason? Did you know that your garage was a crematory? Were you cleaning up in such a hurry to destroy what little evidence might be left?"

"What?" Porter shouted. "Jordan, are you crazy?"

"Your garage fire was arson! A carefully planned fire to burn up the body of Slats Meegan. Nothing was left of him but the 'slats' from his corset!"

Porter turned pleadingly to Anderson. "Inspector, this screwball's gone far enough."

Anderson sighed. "Hear him out, Mr. Porter. Maybe he is bats."

Marc advanced on Miriam and planted himself in front of her.

"I'd like you to hear the story of four bullets, Miriam. Please listen.

"Bullet number one came from that hole." Marc pointed an accusing finger at the rent in the davenport. "I dug it out myself.

"Bullet number two came from a cash box hidden in Meegan's room. I suspect it's one he used for a murder he's supposed to have committed years ago.

"Bullet number three was dug out of the shoulder of Miss Trixie Donovan! She was shot last night a few minutes after talking to me.

"Bullet number four I fired in this house, this afternoon, from a gun I found tangled up in a pair of your panties! Just a minute!" Marc held up a restraining hand as she stiffened against the cushion, and inhaled a gasping breath. "Hear the rest.

"Know what Miss Donovan told me last night? I've known you a long time. Nora's known you longer. Yet never a word of the fact that you're illegitimate. Phenomenal that such a secret could be kept. It must've been very important to you. Trixie Donovan knew the secret, and Meegan found out from her. Your money's all gone, isn't it, Miriam? You were being blackmailed by Meegan, weren't you? Publicity about your doubtful parentage was the sword over your head. Running out of money, Meegan got tough, and you got desperate.

"Dolly somehow found out. You had two reasons to kill her: she stole your boy friend; she knew your secret. So you bopped her with a rolling pin while she was taking a dose of pepsin, tucked her into her car, and drove to the crossing. You took along a pair of Joel's overshoes to cover your footprints, if any. You made those wobbly prints back to Ted's car.

"The trouble was, Ted saw you and followed. So you drove his car back here. You slipped! You should have locked his car and taken the keys back to the wreck!

"When Meegan got rough, shot at you, kidnaped you, you planned his death too. You burned him! You stripped him of his gun and—you thought—all telltale metal objects. But you forgot the 'slats' in his corset! It was a fatal oversight, Miriam."

"Very clever, Marc," said a low voice. "Very clever."

Marc spun around and froze in his tracks. He was gazing into the ugly black hole of a gun pointed unswervingly at his nose.

He took a step forward. A streak of flame and a thunderclap burst from the gun. Chips of plaster tickled the back of his neck.

"Don't move," cautioned Cynthia coolly. "It's loaded, and I can shoot. That goes for the rest of you too." Her narrow eyes darted around the room. "I demand a promise from each of you. The alternative is a bullet. You are going to promise that none of this reaches anyone outside this room. Speak up."

She covered the room with her eyes and the muzzle of the gun. The silence was overwhelming.

"All right—who refuses to promise?"

"But, Mrs. Porter, I got my duty," protested Anderson. "Homicide—"

"Put it this way. If it doesn't run counter to your duty, will you promise?"

Anderson hesitated. "Yes, ma'am. Guess I can do that."

"You have it nearly right, Marc." Cynthia's voice was calm and icy. "Except for one small detail. Miriam had nothing to do with it! Get that. She knew nothing about it! I hid the gun in her dresser so that Don wouldn't find it. Those are old clothes of hers that she never wears.

"Meegan was blackmailing *me*, not Miriam! He'd taken my money, and I'd borrowed all Miriam's. What a time I had trying to explain why I needed it! He called the day of the party, the fool, and Dolly let him in. He thought she was Miriam, and spilled the beans. So I had to kill her. She'd never have kept the secret.

"Ted was an accident, Marc. He almost caught me.

"I had to kill Meegan too, finally. He got too rough. He was frightening me indirectly, through Miriam. When he kidnaped her, I saw red, literally. I couldn't go on. If the police had caught him, I'd have confessed the whole thing, ended it. I couldn't risk endangering Miriam any more. But when she was released, there was still a chance to wipe out Meegan and Trixie. Stamping on a couple of vermin seemed saintly. I'm sorry I missed her!"

"Cynthia," said Marc quietly, "what'd you use on Meegan?"

"A rolling pin."

"Why'd you poison Rags with a loaded piece of candy?"

"To make the fire appear arson, by an outsider."

"You knew Meegan was feeding meat to Rags?"

"Yes. So he could call on me, the back way."

Tears ran down her cheeks as she turned to Miriam.

"I've fought all my life to give you a break, dear. I've made a mess of it. Please forgive me!

"And now, Mr. Jordan, you have four bullets. One in the ceiling over your head is five. Let's make it a round half-dozen."

Quick as a tiger, she pressed the muzzle of the gun against her breast and pulled the trigger.

"Marc," Tony asked softly, "did you really think Miriam was guilty?"

Marc extended his coat and pulled it over Nora's shoulder. They huddled on the veranda waiting for a cloudburst to slacken.

He was silent for a time, then said slowly, "At first, yes, on the theory that she was jealous of Dolly. She might have faked the shot, but she didn't fake the kidnaping. And she did something that clinched her innocence: she hid her pin in Meegan's car. Obviously, had she been involved, she'd never have done that. She wouldn't want Meegan to be caught. Finding the gun in her room, though, was a shock!"

With his free hand, Marc squeezed Tony's arm.

"I'm terribly sorry that I was so rough with Miriam. By working on her, I hoped to continue the 'scaring' and get a confession."

Nora shivered.

"Marc," she muttered, "let's get drunk!"

About the Author

Robert Mark Laurenson (1906-1982) wrote three mysteries. He had no training in writing, but after growing so disgusted over one mystery he read, he decided to write a better one. That became his first book, *The Case of the Railroad Murder*.

Laurenson was born in Illinois, and worked as an engineer for railway companies. At the time his second book was published, in 1949, he and his wife lived in Verona, Pennsylvania, where he worked for the Union Switch and Signal Co. From 1949 to 1970, he was the superintendent of communications at the Frisco Railway, working from Springfield, Missouri. After 1970, he retired, but continued consulting for the railway.

His first two books, published with Phoenix Press, featured railway lawyer Marc Jordan. The third, *Better Off Dead*, published with Arcadia House, was a stand-alone mystery.

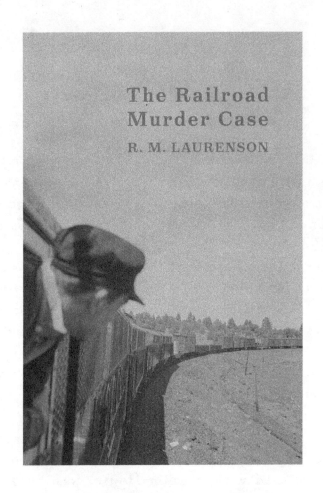

The Railroad
Murder Case

R. M. LAURENSON

**Also Available
Coachwhip Publications
CoachwhipBooks.com**

WHITE

FOR A

SHROUD

DONALD CLOUGH CAMERON

**Also Available
Coachwhip Publications
CoachwhipBooks.com**

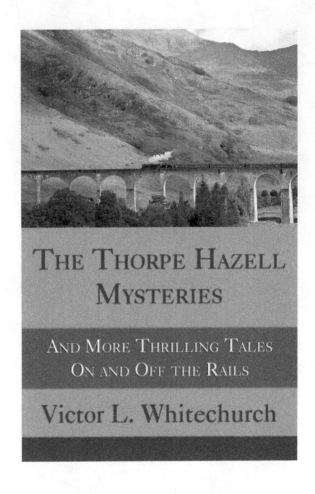

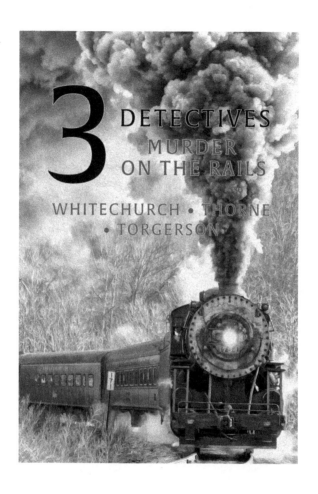

3 DETECTIVES

MURDER ON THE RAILS

WHITECHURCH • THORNE • TORGERSON

Also Available
Coachwhip Publications
CoachwhipBooks.com

THE OWL
SANG
THREE
TIMES

VERA KELSEY

Also Available
Coachwhip Publications
CoachwhipBooks.com

Also Available
Coachwhip Publications
CoachwhipBooks.com

BLOOD-RED DEATH

MINNA BARDON

Also Available
Coachwhip Publications
CoachwhipBooks.com

THE CASE OF THE
ADVERTISED
MURDER

MINNA BARDON

Also Available
Coachwhip Publications
CoachwhipBooks.com

Printed in the USA
CPSIA information can be obtained
at www.ICGtesting.com
LVHW040555101023
760592LV00002B/305